OVERSEAS STORIES

Six Short Stories by

Mitchell Hagerstrom

Penryn Editions 2019

OVERSEAS STORIES

Copyright © 2019 by Mitchell Hagerstrom

Published by

PENRYN EDITIONS

Penryn Editions P.O. Box 167
Queenstown, Maryland 21658

ISBN : 978-1-7330086-2-4

This is a work of fiction. Names, characters, places, and incidents are the product of the author's imagination or are used fictitiously, and any resemblance to actual persons, living or dead, events, or locales is entirely coincidental.

A shorter version of this book with fewer stories was previously published by Tiny Toe Press as a Kindle e-book in 2012.

Cover Photo by Michael Collins

AUTHOR'S NOTE

For five years in the 1980s I lived and worked on the island of Pohnpei in the Western Pacific. My memories of that time were the source of these stories, six overlapping fictions carefully crafted and linked one to another. Together they form a short novel that also serves as a follow-up to my first book, *Miss Gone-overseas,* which was narrated by a fictional woman named Mieko who lived on the same island during WWII. When the war in the Pacific ended, so did that book's narrative. Since the course of the war shaped the plot, it was a natural ending. Still, many readers have asked what happened? What happened is here. However, readers need not have read the first book to enjoy this one.

Overseas Stories opens with a Japanese national who was born on the island and returns to visit in 1975. He visits again ten years later, and he also appears as one of the main characters in the book's last story. The second story gives readers a comic glimpse of his half-sister's home life as she deals with her philandering husband.

In the third story a young native woman gives an American couple a much-appreciated gift. The fourth story is told by a woman who chose to stay behind when her husband left the island. A dead man narrates the fifth story, a tale of an unhappy tourist who makes a choice, and then changes his mind. All three stories have echoes of events in the earlier book, a child who was acquired, a woman who chooses to be left behind, and a suicide.

The book's last story showcases Helen, child of the next generation. She questions her parentage while confronting the puzzles all youth face: who am I and where am I going? Her grandmother gives her the answer to a secret, and during a visit to her uncle in Japan she receives the answer to another secret she didn't even know existed. Also, in Japan Helen gains an unexpected mentor who nurtures her confidence in herself.

Mitchell Hagerstrom, 2019

OTHER WORKS BY MITCHELL HAGERSTROM

"MISS GONE-OVERSEAS", Pillow Book 1st
Edition published by Tiny Toe Press in 2012, 2nd
Edition published by Penryn Editions 2019

"GATHERED PIECES, short narratives
published by Penryn Press 2019.

CONTENTS

SAME FATHER, DIFFERENT MOTHER

In his limited English, Shige described as best he could the women he was seeking: Armina, an older woman, and her daughter Mariko who would now be in her early thirties. The hotel clerk shook his head, said he'd never heard of them. With the clerk's help, Shige filled out the form for a rental car. He then explained he wanted to find the old Japanese hydroelectric plant. The clerk gave him a local map and marked the roads for him.

Although the town was different, Shige thought it had not grown very much. He had no problem finding the roads he needed, and after turning inland before the bridge, the landscape began to look familiar. He pulled off the road next to a large stand of bamboo, thinking the house should be there, right on the river. But he found no signs of a house. He waded through the underbrush, finding nothing man-made at all except an odd waist-high stack of rocks, a monument of some sort. Still, he was sure the house had been there.

Instead of leaving, he rolled up his pant cuffs and found a rock at river's edge on which to perch. Cooling his feet in the water, he gazed up into the high canopy of trees shading the banks of the river. Birds he couldn't see, too small or too shy, twittered back and forth to each other, perhaps discussing among themselves his intrusion into their home territory. When he drove on to the old hydroelectric plant, he found it was a derelict.

From the hotel veranda the next day, Shige watched as an old man stooped to insert cuttings in the damp ground beside the walkway. Assuming they were meant to be a hibiscus hedge, as the island was rife with them, Shige called down a greeting and the old man responded in Japanese. "What color will they be?" Shige asked.

"Red," the old man answered, then squinted up toward the sky. "Soon will be rain," he said.

Shige laughed. "Soon will be rain," he repeated, remembering from his childhood the uncountable gray days and the thundering noise of rain on the metal roof. And more: he remembered the myriad hues of green that make up an island landscape, and the vast cloud-laden sky on non-rainy days, and that here there were more stars in the night sky than anywhere else in the world.

Shige had been born on this island during Japanese colonial times. He left during the war, entrusted to the care of other evacuees during the voyage to the home islands. Shige's father, the engineer in charge of the colony's main hydroelectric plant, stayed behind, and the two were reunited in the homeland at war's end. Shige never forgot his day of leaving: the tearful goodbyes, the departing ones ladened with *leis* and *mwaramwars*. For days the sweet scent of flowers filled the ship's cabins and corridors.

Shige's return visit to the island had been prompted by his father's death and what he had learned during the gloomy task of sorting through the papers in his desk. First, there was a ledger detailing money sent to the island to support what appeared to be a child left behind, a child named Mariko. Shige's father had never told him about any such child, nor had he ever spoken about Armina, who had been Shige's nanny and who was evidently the mother of the child. The second find was a notebook, similar to a diary, with the name Mieko on the inside cover. She apparently had come to the island as a brothel worker.

As Shige read through the notebook of this unknown woman, he was surprised to find a description of himself and his father making their farewells on his day of leaving, the day he remembered with all the flowers. His father appeared again in the notebook's later pages, not by name but as the engineer, and not as a client of the brothel but as a friend of the governor general who had become a permanent guest there. Shige vaguely remembered the governor general and his extreme girth.

The notebook he found ended on the first day of the American bombings, and it suggested a small group comprising the journal's narrator and another woman who was the manager of the brothel, along with the governor general and a young corporal had plans to go to the engineer's house on the river, the house where Shige was born and raised. In their post-war years together, Shige's father had never spoken of any of these people, people who must have arrived at his father's house or how else did the notebook survive and his father acquire it?

All these thoughts and memories had been triggered by the hotel gardener telling him the blooms would be red, as red had been Armina's favorite color. Accepting the elderly gardener's wisdom and his prediction of coming rain, Shige borrowed a hotel umbrella and then started off on foot, heading toward Waterfront Road. On the way, he passed the location of his primary school and the adjacent religious shrine, but all that remained were some entrance posts and some worn stone steps leading to nothing.

The day before, after his drive to the river, Shige had walked in the other direction as far as the old Nambo Department Store. The sturdy concrete hulk of the building was now being used as a government mechanical shop. He remembered as a child being dazzled by the glamour and glitz of the Nambo's display cases, their mirrors enhancing the appeal of the offerings. Mieko's notebook mentioned shopping in the Nambo and visiting the rooftop, a popular gathering place in the evenings. Shige noted that she had neglected to tell about the monkey kept in a cage up there, but maybe it was gone by the later years of the war.

On this day, walking in the other direction, Shige came to the Protestant Church, built during Japanese times. The churchyard was still filled with fine old jacaranda trees that in season bloom the same delicate color as Japanese wisteria. He also noted the church still hosted services. Farther along the same street he studied the various small shops lining the road and could not help comparing them to his childhood days when the establishments on this same stretch of road seemed more prosperous.

Taking a different route back to his hotel Shige discovered a small building on the main street that housed the tourist bureau. There, he was relieved to find the young woman behind the counter spoke Japanese. He began describing the woman named Armina, who had been his nanny, and her daughter who would be a grown woman herself, and who he believed was his sister.

The young woman started laughing, held up her hands and would not let him continue. "Wait, wait," she said, "let me get my supervisor." As her supervisor did not speak Japanese, she translated, and Shige learned her supervisor was the husband of the child Mariko, now called Maria. Valerio, his new-found brother-in-law, threw open his arms in welcome and whisked Shige into his car and drove the few blocks to his wife's establishment.

Although his father's bookkeeping did not state explicitly that the child, he was sending money for, was his own, when Maria and Shige met, he knew instantly that they shared the same father. The gestures, that certain tilt of the head, and each shared a dimple only on the left side. However, their first meeting was awkward. She had been interrupted during the afternoon cleaning of her lunchroom and was apparently embarrassed being caught dressed as a scrubwoman with a kerchief tied around her hair.

Shige was not fluent in English, and Maria's Japanese was sketchy, but they managed. When she learned Shige would only be on-island one more day, she invited him to dinner that night at her home. Valerio obliged with marking the directions on Shige's tourist map. Maria told him to look for the house under a large flame tree, a house with a deep red-colored front door.

Shige had no problem finding the house and the evening started well. His sister was an excellent cook and a gracious hostess. He thought the house tastefully furnished, and the two daughters, a toddler and a pre-teen were well behaved. Helen, the older of the two girls, spoke Japanese fairly well, but with an odd accent. Seated next to her father, she acted as his translator. Shige suspected, though, from the girl's fair coloring, that Valerio was not her true father.

Although the evening began pleasantly. Armina, his childhood nanny, was dressed dramatically, like a Kabuki dancer, Shige thought. Her long red dress had a high, ruffled neckline and her face was dusted pale with powder, lips painted a brilliant red, dark hair piled high in an elaborate knot, held there with ornate hair sticks. She was haughty and dismissive, nothing like the lively young woman Shige remembered. When he talked about the notebook he found in his father's desk and mentioned some of the people in it, Armina denied knowing any of them. She all but accused him of fabricating the notebook. Shige regretted he had not brought it with him. When he tried to tell her about the small piece of writing at the end in his father's hand, Armina abruptly left the table. The evening ended with quiet embarrassment and apologies.

Early the next morning Maria called Shige's hotel and left a message asking if he would come that morning to her place of business so they could talk. When he arrived, she apologized again for her mother's rudeness. The pair then spent a few hours together, managing with broken Japanese and broken English, to get to know each other. The awkwardness of the conversation made Shige promise himself he would enlist help upon his return home to improve his English.

Still, he and Maria managed to share information of their childhoods. He began with the house on the river, which Maria did not remember, and the old couple, Gustof and Santa, who Maria did remember and had called uncle and auntie. Although his father's ledger named her as Mariko, she did not remember being called anything but Maria. She admitted her name may have been westernized, and that her mother always called her Mari-chan.

She had been too young to remember the

move into town, into what she was later told had once been a ryokan, or small Japanese inn, once belonging to Armina's Japanese father. It was on the water side of Waterfront Road and had suffered only minor damage in the war. Maria said Armina did speak some English, even before she found work as a maid for an American missionary family. Maria never knew where her mother had learned it.

Later, when Maria started school, Armina with the help of Santa and Gustof established a small carry-out lunch business for workers who commuted into town. When Maria was a teenager, her mother officially opened the *ryokan* as a small hotel. Sometimes American government officials stayed there when the rest of the island accommodations were full. And in the late 1960s the clientele was mostly hippie world trekkers or Peace Corps kids assigned to the outer villages who came into town looking for a cheap place for R&R.

Shige, in turn, told her how when he was evacuated the ship did not deliver the colonists to the homeland. Instead, all had been offloaded on Saipan.

There, the citizens of Garapan, the island's main town, were required to house these uninvited visitors. Shige was assigned to a carpenter and his family.

The carpentry shop occupied the main floor, living quarters above, and Shige's bed was placed in the bottom of a cabinet in the shop. The family was not stingy, merely pressed for space as they had three children, all girls. The carpenter seemed pleased to have a pseudo-son to teach, and for over a year, Shige had been pleased to play the role of that son. Shige then told Maria that he had continued in that trade because he was so grateful to that family.

He was there in the summer of 1944 when the bombardment of Saipan began. The screams of terrified neighborhood women were almost louder than the sounds of the bombing. Quickly, his host family packed what they could carry, and fled. Shige chose to hide. He crept into his sleeping cabinet, slid the doors shut and in all the chaos he was not missed by his fleeing family.

After the bombardment, when the American soldiers drove their jeeps into Garapan and offered sweets to the children, Shige was among them and remembers that the chocolate bars, in such a hot climate, were melted and sticky, but the children were happy to lick the dark sweet off the paper. Shige's host family were never found. Like the others who fled, they must have jumped to their deaths from the Saipan cliffs onto the rocks and sea below.

Maria shook her head at the story. "The Americans would not have killed the civilians," she said. "It had been a fear here, too," she said, "but it did not happen."

Maria looked up to a signal from the kitchen and told Shige she needed to attend to her work. He asked if he could take Helen to lunch as his flight was late in the day. Maria agreed and called the school to alert them. It turned out to be a splendid idea.

When Shige picked her up Helen said she wanted to go to a place quite a ways from the town, a place that had excellent hamburgers. Shige chuckled to himself, already admiring her spunk, and he thoroughly enjoyed the long drive over a potholed dirt road, an exhilarating adventure of thumping along with the jungle closing in on both sides. His niece was a delightful companion, and as she said, the hamburgers were excellent. On parting, the pair agreed to become pen pals, an agreement they enjoyed for many years.

Ten years later, Shige pays another visit to the island. Leaving the hotel, he takes one of the hotel umbrellas from the rack before setting off in his rented car. Maria had called, an unusual occurrence, and said Armina wanted to see him and he has flown here for that purpose. Maria cautioned him her mother is not well.

On the way, to kill time as he's early and for something cooling, he stops at a place that sells ice cream. The woman behind the counter who hands him the cone is Western, and Shige recalls the Belgian girls and their family who had been interned during the war. He wonders if this woman was one of the three Belgian sisters. To his small bow and thank-you, she answers he is welcome. Had his English been better, he might have noticed her accent and pondered the fact that English speakers have as many different dialects and accents as are found in Japan. He then remembers the name written in the ledger concerning the transfer of money to the island for the left-behind daughter. Shige looks up at her and says the name, hesitantly as he is not sure of the pronunciation. The woman nods, smiles, and repeats the name. He returns her smile and lifts his ice cream cone as if in a toast. Now it is all so clear. In the years after the war when the island infrastructure was in disrepair, it was possible to transfer credit via commercial enterprises. And, of course, the head of the Belgian family enterprises and the island's hydroelectric engineer would have known each other.

At his sister's house, a maid answers and shows him in. He leaves his *zori* and enters barefoot. No slippers are provided but the tile floor is clean and delightfully cool underfoot. The maid shows him into the living room or parlor and, in a mix of English and the local language, offers to bring him coffee. He declines, with a small bow.

Against one wall is a large aquarium with small, iridescent blue fish, a miniature school of them flitting back and forth, darting in and out of a large clump of white coral. Against another wall is a bookcase with small framed photographs displayed along the top: formal portraits of the two daughters, Shige's nieces. Helen, the older of the two, is now a student in Hawaii. Over the years she and Shige have exchanged brief letters and holiday cards. Then a photo of Maria and her husband Valerio with what appears to be the Golden Gate Bridge in the background. Then an old black and white, slightly out of focus, of a young woman wearing a white dress, such as a maid or a nurse might wear, and the face of a small child peering out from behind her skirts. Shige assumes they are Armina and his sister Maria.

From the kitchen comes the sound of the maid singing to herself. He wanders over to the sliding glass door and looks out into the garden and across the estuary to the town of Kolonia. He slides the door open and steps down onto the matted floor of a covered lanai. Not tatami, of course, but a native weaving of pandanus.

Maria has told him that her mother says she now remembers that the governor general and his corporal came to live at the house on the river.

He hears the sliding glass door opening and turns to see the maid helping Armina down the two small steps. Quickly, he goes to take her other arm and together they lead her to one of the rattan chairs. Her hair no longer black, is twisted into a scanty grey topknot. She wears a white Chinese-style tunic, gray trousers, and embroidered slippers. Seated, she says something to the maid, and then motions for Shige to pull his chair closer to hers.

Shige begins to sit, then half rises from his chair to bow. He's so nervous his greeting sticks in his throat.

Armina waves her hand as if brushing aside a mosquito or an annoying fly. "What did you expect, Shige-chan? Old women do nothing but get older." Her voice harsh, but Shige is relieved to see the hint of a smile.

The maid returns and hands Armina a fan and

the scarf Shige had sent, one of those absurdly expensive, colorless silk scarves scribbled over and over with a designer's signature. Armina brings it to her nose, sniffs, then drapes it over her shoulders. "A very nice present," she says and opens the fan.

Shige begins a proper protest, an apology for such a humble gift, but Armina hushes him, flicks her fan at him. "I tire quickly," she says.

Shige sits back, and Amina returns to slowly fanning herself. Again, the glass door slides open and the maid brings a tray with iced drinks. "Limeade," Armina says, and motions for the maid to set the tray on the low table nearby.

"Now," she says when the maid leaves, "I will tell you about the governor general and his corporal. You must understand that I did not remember them before because they were with us such a short time. They came after the first bombing."

"You never met these people?" Shige asks.

Armina fans herself furiously. "Is it usual," she says, "to present a pregnant wife to gentlemen guests? You must remember your father kept a proper

Japanese household."

Shige nods.

"Now," she says, "listen, and do not interrupt. They came, as I said, after the first bombing. The governor general died during a later bombing. A heart attack, your father said. And the corporal? He left to rejoin the other soldiers."

Shige interrupts: "and there were no women?"

Armina snaps the fan shut and shakes it at Shige. "I tell you," she says, "there was only the governor general and his corporal."

"I have been to where the house was," Shige says, "and I saw there a high pile of stones that perhaps mark a grave."

"Yes," Armina says, "the governor general's grave." She reopens the fan. The glasses of limeade sit untouched and sweating.

Shige is disappointed with the visit and does not stay on. He takes the first flight out, a window seat. When the plane banks he can see the rooftops of the town, then across the estuary to his sister's house. Then the wings level out, and he sees the dark mountain tops, and then only ocean and sky. When the stewardess stops her trolley in the aisle, Shige asks for a scotch and water.

Armina had acknowledged two of the people from the diary but not the woman who wrote it. Why had she asked him to come all this way for something that could be written in a letter? When Shige met Maria's daughters ten years ago, Helen was almost fluent in Japanese. She said her grandmother had taught her, that it was the "at home" language when she was growing up. But as Helen had never been taught to write it, over the years she wrote to him in English and Rose, Shige's housekeeper, translated and then wrote return letters for him. Rose is fluent in several languages, and he understands calling her merely a housekeeper is absurd. She is much more than that.

Another sip of scotch and Shige nearly chokes when he realizes what was so odd about Armina: her Japanese was that of a mountain dialect. Neither she, nor Maria, nor Helen has a Tokyo accent. How could that be? Shige's father was born and raised in Tokyo, and all the women in his household would also have a Tokyo accent, meaning the woman who calls herself Armina is a fraud.

Then there is the fragment of writing Shige found tucked in the pages near the end of the notebook. It was in his father's hand. An odd piece of writing, Shige thought, as if someone were relating a dream:

I made a fire of sticks and some embers from the kitchen. When she came from the house, she knelt near the fire and sat back on her heels.

I asked if she had changed her mind. She shook her head and handed me a notebook with papers spilling out.

I took it and sifted out the loose papers. One was a photograph of two boys in school uniforms.

My brothers, she said. She took it and the loose pages from me and began tossing them onto the fire. Tear the pages out, she said, nodding toward the notebook. They will burn better that way.

Instead, I opened the notebook and began to read. She grabbed for it, but I held it out of her reach.

Burn it, she said.

No, I want it as a memento.

Don't be foolish. It's nothing.

Still, I would like to keep it.

Will you promise to never read it?

Now, who would make a promise like that?

You won't find it very interesting, she said. She took the remaining loose papers, leaned forward and placed them on the fire. Now, she said, I'm dead. Good riddance. We watched as the fire consumed the paper.

The light was fading. At the river's edge, I disrobed and placed my clothing on a dry stone, her notebook and my glasses on top. I knelt and she poured water over me from a bucket, then soaped me, then poured more water over me. I stepped into the shallows and found my usual small boulder, a comfortable perch chest-high in the water. After she washed herself, she settled on a nearby boulder.

Under the canopy of trees, the light was going fast, and I remember the water felt colder than usual.

She said she wanted to wash the smell of smoke from her hair, but complained it was too late, that her hair would not dry.

I agree, I said, it is too late, too late for everything.

Now you are being an odd person, she said.

She loosened her hair and lowered herself into the water until completely submerged, then jumped, her body half out of the water and twisting, the spray from her hair flying in an arc. Without my glasses, I saw only a pale blue. *Already she was a ghost.*

UNDER THE FLAME TREE

When Geneva arrives back at the hotel, the clerk hands her the key to her bungalow and a note, an invitation to dinner from Valerio's wife. Come early if you can, Maria had written, and the directions to the house: the road to town, turn right at the last street before the bridge, then about a quarter mile down on the left. Watch for a large flame tree.

Geneva arranges a hotel jeep for the evening, then walks up the path to her bungalow. After hanging her grey linen in the bathroom to steam, she showers and shampoos the saltwater from her hair. She still feels a bit wired from the day's outing: sharks! Would anyone back home believe it?

When she turns just before the bridge, she sees the sun has begun its descent behind the far ridge of Sokehs. The flame tree, at the height of its seasonal flowering, is easy to spot. She pulls up and parks behind Valerio's sedan. The tree's wide limbs cast a cool, green, underwater shadow on the pale-yellow residence. Valerio stands on the porch beside a deep-red front door. He flips his cigarette away as Geneva approaches.

She notes the print of his shirt: white cranes on a deep blue background. Some standing on tall, spindly legs, others flying, their wide wings fluttering across his chest. He gives her the same smile as the first time they met, displaying his strong, wholesome, but crooked teeth. She had decided back then that modern orthodontics would have taken away half his charm.

"You mustn't look at me like that," she says. "You mustn't watch me tonight." She steadies herself with a hand on his arm and begins to loosen the strap of her sandal.

"Leave them on," he tells her. "Maria makes an exception for dinner parties. Shoes are allowed in the house. Come, she's waiting out back."

Geneva heels click loudly on the tile floor as she follows him past the living room where a long aquarium glows against one wall and where thirteen-year-old Leialoha sprawls across one of the rattan sofas, turning the pages of a magazine. She wears earphones attached to a Walkman and does not look up.

Only a few days ago Geneva had studied this child from across one of the hotel dining tables while everyone played their charade of Sunday brunch *en famille*. Silent Leialoha with the sulky, sultry beauty of a Gauguin ingenue who asked her father to order her a Tab float, but otherwise said nothing. And Maria had turned to Geneva and said, "I have been wanting to meet you, and then I find you are already Valerio's friend."

It was then that a loud scream filled the room

and every table turned to see the American ambassador's wife standing, her chair tumbled back on the floor, and the woman beating at her skirt. Apparently, a gecko had fallen from the rafters and mistaken her leg for an escape route.

Now Geneva's heels clickety-click behind Valerio as he waits for her beside a set of glass doors. "Go on," he says, as he slides one open. "I'll be out in a minute."

The lanai faces west, with a view of the town across the estuary, but protected from the glare of the setting sun by the Sokehs ridge. Geneva recognizes this particular vantage point as one she has seen on postcards, which is not a coincidence since Valerio happens to be the State Director of Tourism.

She finds Maria reclining on a chaise on the far side of the lanai, elegant in a crisp white dress with a high collar and a flounced hem. "I'm so glad you're finally here," Geneva says, her glossy dark hair pulled back in a low chignon and a yellow hibiscus tucked behind one ear. She looks like a print in the Paul Jacoulet book Geneva has seen for sale at the hotel.

"I'm afraid I'm unfashionably early," Geneva says.

"Not at all. I was afraid you would not come, that you would think my invitation too spur of the moment. Please, sit down." Maria indicates the other chaise. "A ship from the south arrived recently bringing New Zealand lamb and I hate to keep it frozen for very long. Anyway, having a party and inviting you seemed a good way to keep my husband home tonight."

Geneva colors and hopes the bit of sun she had taken that day conceals it. She crosses her legs. "I really don't know why I packed linen," she says, smoothing the front of her skirt." She is normally good at party small talk, but Maria's remark totally unnerved her.

"Ah, yes," Maria says. "Tourists come to our little third-world backwater for adventure and then are disgruntled when they find there are no dry cleaners, no golf courses, no high-end shops, no limousine service."

"Actually," Geneva says, "wrinkled linen has become quite fashionable. But I wasn't raised that way.

To me, wrinkled linen always seems ... unironed."

They hear the swish of the door, and then Valerio is there, presenting a tray of gin and tonics. When they all have a glass in hand, he raises his. "Ginto," he says, clicking his against theirs. "Ginto," the women echo.

Maria turns to Valerio: "I was just about to ask Geneva about her day's outing." And then to Geneva: "They told the boy I sent with the invitation that you had gone on an outing."

Geneva moves her legs and Valerio sits down on the edge of her chaise. "It was wonderful," she says. "We saw sharks!"

"See!" Maria says. "I told you, Valerio. You should put sharks in your brochures. Tourists love sharks. Tell us, Geneva, how many did you see?"

Geneva inhales and releases a long breath before beginning. "The hotel tour boat took us out to that atoll ..." When she pauses, Valerio says the name and she nods, then continues, "We were snorkeling just before the passage into the lagoon, along the wall of the reef. The water was deep, but I could make out at least five sharks, maybe a dozen. Their tails were swaying from side to side, but they were stationary."

"Yes," Valerio says. "The outgoing tide was making the water flow out of the lagoon, and the sharks had to swim to stay in place. That's how they sleep."

As Geneva listens, she takes a sip of her drink. "Interesting," she says. "There may have been even more, but farther down and very shadowy. Then a boat full of Japanese tourists arrived. They were fishing, and when they began chumming, our guide told to us get out of the water. Fast."

"Yes," Valerio says, shaking his head. "A shark took one of my uncle's arms."

"How awful," Geneva mutters.

"He was cleaning fish over the side of the boat and did not see it coming. It was good you got out of the water. I need to find out who was chumming when there were snorkelers or divers in the water. I'll ask your hotel to check with your guide. I can get that outfit banned from taking people out to the atoll."

There was the sound of a vehicle pulling up out front.

"I'll go," Maria says, getting up. "We can have another drink inside. The mosquitos will be out soon."

The door slides open and shuts behind her.

"Such a lovely view," Geneva says.

"Then you're not sorry you came?"

"She knows, damn it."

Valerio shrugs. "It's a small island. It would be cruel not to tell her."

"Did she know last Sunday? Did she? I must say she behaves very well. Do you always tell her?" Geneva tries to keep her voice to a whisper, but there is an uncontrollable shrillness to it. "Please," she says, "go on in. I'll be there in a minute."

"Then you are not sorry you came?"

"Go on," she says. "Watching the sunset from here is everyday for you, but not for me."

He nods and leaves.

She settles back on the chaise. The ridge behind the town hides what is probably a spectacular sunset, such as what she sees from the hotel veranda.

Here, the smooth surface of the estuary merely turns a muddy gold. The town is in shadow, and lights are being turned on here and there, tiny pinpoints, like the sparkle of glowworms on the floor of the dark jungle landscape. It was the way the island looked the night she arrived. In less than a week, she will be leaving.

She gets up and goes inside where Valerio hands her another drink. Leialoha has vacated the rattan sofa. Maria introduces her to Simon Luke and his wife Serlina, and Dr. Howard Olson, the American doctor Geneva has noticed before at the hotel, always dining alone at a place set at the bar. Simon Luke is a tall young man with large ears. He looks to be in his late twenties and has an important position as State Director of Finance. His wife Serlina is perched on exceedingly high heels, no doubt to compensate for her husband's great height. Her long sparkling earrings framed her pretty face.

At the table, Geneva is surprised at the sophistication of Maria's menu: roasted leg of lamb properly pink and expertly sliced, a gratin of breadfruit, steamed wing beans, and a salad of sliced banana flowers with hearts of palm, the vinaigrette lightly sweetened with pineapple juice, and all served by a Filipino houseboy. In addition to a basket of *lavash* and small bowels of real butter. Maria has a popular lunch place in town, but the dinner menu makes it obvious, to Geneva at least, that she knows more about cooking than just making sandwiches and such.

The wine is Australian, and the conversation, after the appreciative comments about the food, soon lapses into films. For Geneva and Dr. Olson, Valerio explains that the very latest videos travel quickly to the island and almost every household with electricity has a viewing device.

Even before settling in the dining room, during drinks before dinner it was obvious the assembly of people had very little in common. At the table, Geneva has been seated next to Dr. Olson. His recent arrival on the island quite apparent by his pale skin and sunburned nose, but Geneva cannot not help noticing he has beautiful blue-green eyes.

He turns to her. "I've seen you at the hospital. Claire told me you were here to check the pharmacy accounts."

Geneva nods. "I've been here three weeks, making sure the books here match with the figures on the invoices that were sent to D.C."

"And?" he asks.

"Everything looks fine." She almost suggests they have dinner together some evening at the hotel, but feels Valerio leaning over her shoulder with the wine bottle. She shakes her head, and laughs. Her glass is still full.

Across the table Serlina chatters like a myna bird, fluttering her hands for emphasis, and setting her sparkling earrings to dancing. Her knowledge of the private lives of movie and TV stars is astounding. Her husband says nothing at all, and Geneva begins to zone it all out.

At the hotel, she usually eats an early dinner and retires to her bungalow to read one of the paperback thrillers selected from the shelf behind the hotel reception desk, discards from previous guests.

Sometimes Valerio will come after she has fallen asleep, and he often does not leave until almost dawn. If he comes early-ish they might go down to the bar for a drink or to share a piece of coconut cream pie.

Tonight, Valerio pours glass after glass of wine and the Filipino keeps the sideboard continuously supplied with open bottles. Geneva hears Maria say: "You can take the boy out of the village, but you cannot take the village out of the boy. Especially one who carries the pitiful name of Demasiado Amor."

Geneva has missed the context of this as Dr. Olson was whispering to her: "If I were your husband, I would not have let you come here alone."

Geneva turns to him with raised eyebrows. His remark leaves her speechless. "Let? Let?", she is unable to form a polite response. She glances to her right, to the end of the table, and the white crane wings across the front of Valerio's shirt seemed suddenly menacing.

After dinner, Maria serves coffee and Belgian chocolates in the living room. Dr. Olson leaves directly after dinner, begging forgiveness and explaining he has an early shift the next morning. "I expected Claire to be here," he says to Maria. She whispers something back to him. Geneva can't hear but she can count. Her late invitation is to fill Claire's empty chair. She feels a fool.

Maria and Serlina are sitting together on the rattan love seat. From across the room, Geneva hears Serlina offer her condolences on the recent death of Maria's mother. They also talk about Helen, who seems to be another daughter, and who had come home from school in Hawaii to be with her grandmother for a week or so near the end. How odd Geneva thought, that Valerio has never mentioned he had another daughter, or that there had been a recent death in the family.

Valerio and Luke are having a murmured conversation, and as soon as she judges polite, Geneva stands to say her goodbyes. Valerio walks her out to the jeep. Moonlight has drained the landscape of all color except for the muted red of the flame tree flowers. The ground is littered with the bruised blossoms, once a bright vermillion, now a dull red.

"I don't like your Dr. Olson," Valerio tells her, his voice deep and threatening.

"I hardly spoke to him at all," Geneva answers. "Besides, he's not *my* Dr. Olson. Your wife invited him. Please, don't be so ...," her sentence goes unfinished as Valerio shoves her roughly against the side of the hotel jeep, and pulls up her skirt.

"If I had a knife," he says, "I would cut you here." His fingers pinch her high on her inner thigh. "I would make a mark that would never go away." He then pinches so hard she lets out a cry which he smothers with a kiss.

Driving back to the hotel, her inner thigh still throbbing with pain, she thinks about going home. The *mark* he gave her will be nothing but a bad bruise and gone in a week or so. She imagines dining out for years on the story about the sharks, how she floated above them while they slept. Meanwhile, she will advise her D.C. friends to avoid packing linen if they sign on to take assignments in third world backwaters.

BLUE DAMSELS

Although Howard is six months into his two-year tour for Public Health, he's still not used to the realities of his assignment to this small island in the middle of the Western Pacific. The hospital is far from U.S. standards with its walls of peeling paint, a leaky roof, not enough sheets for all the beds, no air-conditioning on the wards, no dietitian or functioning kitchen, a rationing of meds, and so on.

Today, he sits at the desk outside ER and begins to log in the pertinent details of his last patient, as young female approaches. In her arms she holds a baby swaddled in a faded beach towel. Howard pauses long enough to point his pen toward the door to the exam room, then quickly finishes his notations: female, approx. 40 years old, multiple burns on face, chest, arms. As neither she nor her family spoke much English, and Howard's knowledge of the local language is far from fluent, it is not clear if the cause was a grease fire or if a kerosene stove exploded. He writes grease fire.

Before joining the young woman in the exam room, he glances down the corridor at the group of women waiting for the Well-Baby Clinic to open. There are no chairs or benches. The women sit on the floor and lean back against the wall. Some are cradling infants, some with small children who languish against their laps. They form an island still-life, utterly quiet and motionless except for the arms of a few of the women who attempt to stir the heavy, humid air by waving sweat-dampened hankies or small towels.

When Howard enters the exam room, he finds the young woman bent over the table and unwrapping the child. As she frees the child's arms from the swaddling, the child reaches up and dislodges the comb anchoring her hair. Howard reaches out, an automatic gesture, some instinct to catch falling objects. But her comb clatters to the floor, and he finds his hands full of her warm, dark hair.

Embarrassed, he drops his hands. While the young woman crouches to retrieve her comb, Howard turns to the child, now naked, kicking his legs and playing contentedly with his own hands and feet. He notes the child's skin is a bit yellow, but the eyes are clear, so it's not jaundice. He estimates the child's age as at least about 6 months, maybe more. "How is he sick?" he asks the young mother.

She has gathered her hair back into a dark globe and re-anchors it with the comb. "He is not sick," she answers. Her voice is soft, her English quite clear.

"If he's not sick, take him home," Howard tells her.

"I want you to take him," she answers.

"I can't do that. If he's not sick, you must take

him home." "Where is your mother," he asks, "your aunties?"

She shakes her head and tells him they make her crazy. Her mother, her aunties, they all make her crazy.

Howard doesn't ask her to explain. Instead, as he washes his hands, he gives her a lecture over his shoulder of how she is wasting his time, blah, blah, blah.... He leaves the room without looking back.

Down at the end of the corridor, beyond the tableau of women waiting for Well-Baby, he sees his wife. He notes the bright print of Sylvia's *lava-lava*, her pale hair, and shoulders. Dohnis, his replacement, has arrived. Howard nods toward the exam room, tells him to talk to the one in there. "See if you can get her to take the kid to Well-Baby," he says, "or see if you can find her family. She's just a kid herself," he adds.

Before leaving the hospital, Howard checks in with Claire, the director's right hand, on a supply order. And then they're off. Often Claire joins them, but today she can't.

Sylvia packed a picnic and they head down the nearby peninsula to what serves as a beach on this otherwise mangrove-locked island. On the way, Howard notes the blood-red door of the Director of Tourism's house where he attended a small dinner party before Sylvia arrived.

The peninsula road is lined with ivory nut palms and weaves through a jungle landscape of *liana*, breadfruit trees, and ginger, all shaded by a high canopy of mimosas. They pass occasional clearings with tin-roofed or palm-thatched houses, some open-sided pavilions, and all surrounded by carefully tended patches of taro, tapioca, and banana trees. Groups of small children stop their games to wave, and skinny dogs bark.

Howard drives slowly as their third-hand van is missing shocks and the road is full of good-sized potholes. Finally, he makes the last sharp turn and eases to a stop in the blinding sunlight above a small, sandless beach, a pitiful excuse of a beach.

Howard slips off sandals, khakis, and shirt and tucks his wallet under the seat. In just his boxers, he hobbles over the half dozen yards of coral shingle and flies forward into a shallow dive. Beneath the top few inches, the water is cool. He swims across the narrow boat channel and finds a large coral whose nooks and crevices are home to a school of small, iridescent blue damselfish. His other ladies, Sylvia calls them.

He looks up when he hears the arrival of the afternoon flight and watches as the sun-polished fuselage, like liquid silver, descends toward the airport. Then there's the scream of brakes, as the plane disappears behind the mangroves that hide the view of the runway.

Suddenly Sylvia pokes his shoulder, tells him he should use sunscreen. She fights to keep the ends of her *lava-lava* from floating up to the surface. Local fishermen often use the boat channel, so she adheres to local custom regarding modest dress and leaves her bikinis for trips to the more deserted atolls. Through the water, Howard can see the pale moonlight of her thighs.

"How are your ladies," she asks.

"Never mind my ladies," he says, running his

hand up between her legs. He anchors himself on a rock and pulls her on to him.

Normally after a swim, they unfold canvas chairs, sit in the sun, have a picnic and a few beers. But back on their so-call beach, Howard feels a small sprinkle. He gazes up at the sky, trying to judge whether it's just a little liquid sunshine or if they're in for a downpour. Then he hears Sylvia calling his name, repeating it over and over in little yelps. In its diminutive form – Howie – it sounds like the local word for "wait" and for a second, he's confused. He hurries over, expecting she's discovered a centipede.

But what she's found, lying in the cradle of the spare tire, is the child in the faded beach towel. Startled by Sylvia's yelps, he's begun to cry.

They head back down the peninsula and Howard tells her about the earlier incident at ER. The rain becomes a deluge and with the windows rolled up, the van is a stuffy box.

"They'll know what to do at the hospital," Howard tells her. "Someone is sure to know the family."

The child continues to fuss, and Sylvia gives him a knuckle to suck on. She comments on his light skin and they speculate on the unknown half of his parentage.

"Obviously *hapa haole*," she says. "Some tourist? Some contract worker? Poor, poor baby," she croons, "papa's up and gone, poor, poor baby."

The rain has stopped by the time they reach the main road and the blacktop is steaming. Howard pauses before turning right, and when he looks to the left to check for traffic, he sees that Sylvia has unknotted her lava-lava and given the kid a nipple. He's so startled that his foot slips from the clutch and the van stalls.

At the hospital, Sylvia refuses to hand the child over to just anyone. They find Claire but then Sylvia insists on waiting until Justina, one of the Filipina nurses, can be found.

It's early evening when they arrive home. They take turns showering and then sit down to the sandwiches and canned potato sticks Sylvia had packed for the picnic. She says she doesn't feel like cooking.

He asks if she'd rather go out for something and she shakes her head.

The neighbor's dogs start barking at an arrival, either Claire who lives next door, or could be their owners. Sylvia's often comments that she's never known a stupider bunch of dogs.

"Maybe we should get a pet," Howard says. "What about an aquarium? I could fill it with blue damsels." He doesn't suggest a dog.

Sylvia shrugs and gets up, tosses the rest of her sandwich in the trash and gets another beer.

"Let's not talk," she says and goes out onto the porch.

He finishes his sandwich, gets another beer, and joins her. Their place doesn't have a sunset view, instead, the light slowly becomes a deeper and richer gold, and the *ylang ylang* tree in the yard, as though triggered by the diminishing light, releases a cloying perfume.

Soon the mosquitos drive them inside, and they lie in bed, side by side without touching. The small red light of the electric mosquito coil glows dimly on the bedside table. Sylvia whispers his name.

"Someone will come for it," he answers. "Don't worry. They'll find the family."

She tells him: "his mouth was so tiny. He was so gentle, as though he knew it was just pretend."

Howard motions for her to turn over and he caresses her back until she falls asleep.

Later, under the patterning of a light rain on the metal roof, he lies with his hands tucked under the pillow, remembering that elusive moment, the weight and warmth of the girl's dark hair, and the smell of coconut oil.

He's still awake when the island roosters crow the false dawn, but when true morning comes, he's fast asleep. He knows it's late when he finally wakes to Sylvia's high-heeled sandals tap dancing across the linoleum between the closet and the bathroom.

"I'm going out for lunch," she calls to him over her shoulder, "probably Maria's. You wanna come?"

Howard turns over and refuses to open his eyes.

"I'll bring you something. Pulled pork or tuna?" she asks.

"Whatever," he answers. He knows where she is really going is to the hospital to check on that kid.

Later, how much later he doesn't know, it becomes too hot to sleep. His skin itches and the sheets are damp. When he gets up to turn the ceiling fan to high, he hears the dogs barking and Sylvia returning. Howard slips into a pair of shorts and goes to the door. But no, it's a dilapidated pickup with five or six women sitting in the truck's bed. It stops on the downslope of the circular drive and an old man gets out of the cab and calls out a native greeting.

Most of the women then climb down and gather around the front steps, bobbing their heads and repeating the old man's greeting. Two of them come forward and deposit a heavy plastic basin at the bottom of the steps, a basin overflowing with gifts:

cans of mackerel, loaves of bread, bags of rice, a box of laundry soap. And tucked here and there are samples of native home-cooking: fried reef fish, taro balls, and yam cakes.

The old man begins a speech. He's nearly toothless, his face the color and texture of a dried fig. As he speaks, he pulls at the frayed hem of his shorts. The few words Howard can catch are not the important ones,
the ones with compound meanings: marriageable but still single, bad but not responsible due to insanity, and a very ornate form of thank-you.

Suddenly, Howard recognizes the faded bundle held by a woman still sitting in the back of the pickup. He stumbles down the steps. The old man catches his arm and the women press forward, to shake his hand, to pat his back. He's embarrassed that his ability to speak the language is so meager. How does one say: think nothing of it, all in the line of duty?

With all the commotion, the kid starts to cry. The woman holding it makes shushing sounds, but the child cries louder. One of the other women takes it and hands it to someone sitting in the cab.

By making little bows and muttering over and over the extremely polite form of thank-you, Howard maneuvers his way to the passenger side.

The girl's warm, dark hair is neatly coiled and secured by the comb. She fixes on Howard her equally warm, dark eyes. And when she hands the kid to him through the window, he takes him.

"I told them he's yours," she says. "And that you want him."

Meanwhile, everyone has piled back in the truck and when it lurches forward Howard jumps aside to keep his toes from being run over.

Back at the steps, the home-cooked goodies in the basin are beginning to draw flies. With the kid asleep in his arms, Howard sits down to wait for Sylvia. While he waits, he practices bits and pieces of barely remembered lullabies and nursery rhymes, inventing nonsense for forgotten words and lyrics, and he digs through the basin, searching for yam cakes, a local delicacy he's acquired a taste for.

FIELD NOTES

The road to Salvador's is hard and smooth. Potholes have been freshly filled with coral rubble and rolled. I pass the derelict pepper plantation, the unattended vines spiraling up fern logs, many leaning at crazy angles like a battalion of exhausted soldiers.

It's the heart of the dry season, those few short weeks when the rains cease, the sky becomes a glorious blue, and the acacia trees bloom pale gold. The season when conjunctivitis is endemic.

I drive slowly. A pickup passes, the bed full of

islanders returning from jobs in town to their homes in the outlying villages. A cloud of coral dust from the truck's wake coats my windshield, making it opaque. Then a sudden THUMP. At once the front of the car is up and over, and before I can brake, the back wheels follow. I quickly pull off the road. I panic, fearing I have run over a child or someone's dog, but it's only the corpse of a small banana tree, felled the night before by the rainless winds.

Last night I had listened apprehensively as the wind played tricks with the night noises: the snap of twigs, the rasp of palm fronds across the metal roof, and the pandanus scratching at the window screen like the insistent fingernails of a night crawler.

My house is secure, but nightcrawlers can become a nuisance when a woman chooses to live alone. A couple of years ago an elderly expat, an eighty-year-old missionary, was raped. They caught the boy. He had a history of dementia.

When my husband was here and we lived up at Seven Houses, our place was broken into once, but all that was missing besides some food and soft drinks were a hand mirror, my hair-cutting scissors, and a bottle of cologne. Not long after that the banker's place was hit, and they took all his wife's dresses. Blanche claims to have seen her clothes walking around town.

Then there's the old story of the Peace Corps volunteer who was raped. This was years ago. She was out walking in the jungle when a man threatened her with a machete. Many say he just happened to be carrying a machete, a normal jungle tool, when he asked her for a fuck. They say he probably didn't threaten her at all, and she could have easily said, No thanks, not today.

At a certain large breadfruit tree, I turn onto the rutted track that leads to Salvador's family compound. Under a high canopy of trees, I drive through fifty yards of wild ginger brushing the sides of the car, before the track makes a loop through an open area of close-cropped grass bordered by small houses and sheds. Most are of weathered plywood and painted in faded shades of blue and yellow, all with metal roofs topped with a multicolored tumble of bougainvillea, a mix of pink, red, yellow, and magenta, which lend the place a decrepit charm.

I wait, standing beside the car, shading my head with the manila folder of paperwork. It's a job order that needs Salvador's signature. I can see him on the far side of the compound, beneath the bamboo arbor supporting his yam vines. He's wearing khaki shorts and is shirtless. He looks over once but gives no sign of greeting, as though the distance between us is an invisible wall. Perhaps he believes his dark skin is an adequate camouflage in the shadow of the arbor. I watch him turn and say something to the naked little boy beside him, and the child runs off towards the cook shed.

Soon Mercedes, Salvador's wife, comes out. As usual, she is wearing layers of elastic-waisted native skirts with intricate appliqués along the hemline. She has pulled the top skirt up, to cover her breasts which she normally keeps bare in the privacy of the family compound. The naked little boy follows her. A grandson, no doubt.

Salvador, instead of performing his usual

peacock strut across the lawn, has disappeared. He's a vain man who won't let himself be seen with pinkeye.

Mercedes and I give each other the little bows of polite greeting, and I utilize the formal gesture for handing her the manila folder: my right hand offers while the left grazes the bottom of the extended forearm, as though holding back the flowing sleeve of a vestigial kimono. Probably a practice left over from the Japanese, like the custom of no footwear in the house.

"Please," I say. "Please, tell the director there's a broken washing machine at the hospital and he must sign paperwork so it can be fixed."

Mercedes nods. She looks tired to tears and I recall a visit here one morning, drinking tea as Salvador ate his breakfast of cold rice and fish. From where we were sitting, I could watch Mercedes and one of her daughters-in-law at their kitchen tasks: the husking, peeling, chopping, grating, grinding, beating, soaking and squeezing required to convince coconuts, breadfruit, taro, tapioca and yams that they are indeed edible. All done with simple tools and lots of muscle.

Now I tell Mercedes I will be back in the morning for the papers. As I leave, I give a final glance in the rear-view mirror and see the boy reaching for the folder. Mercedes raises it above her head, then smacks him for picking at his eyes.

The late afternoon sun is behind me during the drive home. I pass that felled banana tree which is already turning to mush from other cars and trucks stumbling over it. One curve later, I almost run over a young girl. Her arm is raised, and her thumb turned amateurishly in the wrong direction. I stop and motion for her to get in. It is so rare to see anyone hitchhiking, especially a young girl.

"Paige," she says, naming the communications station as her destination. Then, with unusual boldness, she asks if I have a husband.

I answer with a lift of the eyebrows, which can mean yes, I do. Or it can mean yes, I heard your question. Then she asks where I stay, meaning where do I live. I tell her the district and she settles back in the seat, apparently satisfied. Now, if anyone mentions that American lady, she can say: I know her; she stays at Dolohnier.

At the turn-off to Paige, the girl gets out, thanks me, and closes the door lightly, too lightly, and for the rest of the short drive home, the red panel light stays lit.

My neighbors are a Mokilese family and Howard Olson, one of the hospital's American doctors, and his wife. Howard and Sylvia recently adopted a local child. The houses are privately owned but government issued, these being for hospital workers from off-island. When my husband Amos was here, the public works department had assigned us the place up at Seven Houses, government houses build on the site of the old Japanese airfield, the tarmac only inches below the surface of the soil. An arid place. In Dolohnier there is more privacy, as a wide hedge of hibiscus curtains the houses from the road.

With Amos gone, I no longer have the obligation to prepare regular dinners and I've become quite lazy. I open a can of smoked kippers, jazz it up with chopped onion, mustard, and mayonnaise, and turn it into a spread for crackers which I crisp in a slow oven. A quick shower, then wrap myself in a *lava-lava*, fix a sundowner and, with my crackers and kippers, I settle into a canvas porch chair.

If I place the chair just so, there's a tiny view between the trees: to the ocean, the horizon line, and the sky's sunset colors. I sip my pink gin and watch a lizard sprint across the porch rail, the wings of a dragonfly protruding from either side of its mouth, transforming it into a magical new species ready to take flight.

I daydream of being at my desk at the hospital. *Salvador strolls out from his office and comes up to my desk. He's wearing a cat's grin of some private satisfaction.*

What will you do, he asks, if I cannot give you first place in my heart?

I answer that it is better to be dead than to be loved in the second or third place. He shakes his head and I reconsider: with really important people, I say, it's sometimes impossible to come first.

Again, he shakes his head. Poor Claire, he says,
you seem to have lost heart completely. That's bad. I
prefer you to go on believing as you did before.

I remember being so grateful when I was hired
at the hospital, meaning that with a legitimate job I
could stay on the island without Amos. And I
remember the day Salvador showed me this house.
The ragged curtains, dusty screens, the furry scent of
rodents, a stovetop coated in grease, and a soiled,
battered mattress leaning against the wall. And
Salvador had quietly said to me that my husband was
a foolish man. If he had been married to me, he would
not have let me go.

I turned away and said nothing.

It was Amos who left, not me. Less than six
months after we arrived, Amos quit and left for Saudi.
He came here with certain expectations and for him,
nothing measured up. He hated the place and the
people. Yet I remember, he was the same at Chiang
Mai, the same in Kuala Lumpur, and I have no doubt
he's the same in Saudi.

What would he have said if he'd been traveling on my shoulder today? I can almost hear him. Of the derelict pepper plantation: sheer laziness. Of the director's compound: that Salvador and Mercedes are literally enslaved by the extended family they support, by the large number of unproductive members, the elderly, the children, the unemployed, the unemployable. Of the little hitchhiker and her like: rude, nosey little bastards. Of Salvador's case of the pinkeye: that he should get himself a pair of those mirrored sunglasses, the ones with fuck-you printed across the lens.

When night falls and the mosquitoes drive me inside, I wash up the few dishes, leaving them to dry in the rack. Reaching up to turn off the light, I hear a woman's voice. It sounds like she's calling out *mwarmwar, mwarmwar* – the local word for a woven crown of flowers. It's an odd neighborhood and an odd time of day for someone to be selling flowers.

As I open the back door, the Mokilese dogs

come bounding toward my house, barking their fool heads off.

"Little dog," the woman says.

"Big dogs," I say and reach for the stick I keep by the door. The dogs know it and take off back to their own place.

The woman bends down to look under the house. I realize she's looking for her little lost dog. I also squat down and peer under the house, then shrug, tell her there's only those big dogs around here.

When she leaves, I sit down on the steps. My eyes are smarting, perhaps from the smoke of a nearby cook fire, perhaps from the onset of pinkeye. I feel a sudden, terrible longing for the rainy season, for that certain damp odor the earth gives off just before a deluge, a scent of anticipation, like the musky secretion of an animal in heat, luring and enticing the advancing rainstorm.

SUICIDE IS TIMELESS

December 23, 1987

Dear Mrs. Tovar,

Since speaking to you I have been able to locate several people who knew Jason during his stay here, but I have not found any evidence that he left the island and was back on Guam on the date you mentioned. I spoke, specifically, to Lukas Johns whose card was found among Jason's papers, and to the manager of the Cliff Rainbow Hotel where your son stayed, and to the bartender at Little Micronesia, and to some patrons at the Seven-Seven, the last bar where Jason was seen that night.

Lukas told me he had drinks that night and several times before with Jason at the Palm Terrace. He said Jason seemed like a good kid, always warm and friendly, and did not seem in the least depressed. Lukas said they talked about the coincidence of Jason having worked on a sister-ship of the Priscilla B which had put in here during this past year. Tuna boats calling here are still a rarity. Jason told Lukas that he was just passing through on his way to vacation on the mainland.

The manager of the Cliff Rainbow said Jason usually had lunch or a late breakfast in the dining room and then left for the day. Although the hotel has a bar, Jason was rarely seen there. Rita, whose name and number were among Jason's papers, is a local bar girl, one of several that Jason was seen with. She said she had not seen him in several days.

At Little Micronesia, the bartender said Jason was in and out that night, and that he was quite inebriated. The bartender remembered Jason from previous occasions and said he was always cheerful, except one time when he said he hated his job.

That night, after leaving Little Micronesia, Jason went to the Seven-Seven, a shabby after-hours club near the docks. I talked to a few people who claimed to have been there that night and all said Jason was very drunk and several mentioned he had given away his camera, but none would tell me to whom. It's probable Jason also gave away the gold chain you asked about.

The police on routine patrol early the next morning saw the body hanging from the second-floor balcony of the hotel and cut him down. Jason was pronounced dead on arrival at the hospital. Other than the note we sent you, there were many wadded up pieces of paper on the floor of his room, but the writing on them was completely illegible.

I don't know how useful you will find any of the above. I would suggest that you communicate with your son's former employer on Guam, who told my supervisor, Mr. Landau, that the week before Jason left he had turned down two good job offers, adding that he had noticed in the past a pattern of Jason drinking heavily between crewing assignments. He didn't hang out with crewmates and seemed to be nursing a great sadness.

Enclosed is the other key to Jason's suitcase which was mailed December 19th. When Mr. Landau returns in early January, he will complete the death report. I am sorry the shipping arrangements caused you further anguish. This is the first time our newly opened office has had such a responsibility and I apologize for the ineptness. If there is anything else I can do, or if you have any more questions, however slight they may seem, please do not hesitate to write or call. And please accept my deepest sympathy and my prayers.

Sincerely,
Emiliano Welter
Admin. Assist.
Embassy Kolonia

In the hospital morgue, the door of the upper berth of the refrigerated unit lifts and two people stare in at me. The lady is Claire, assistant to the hospital director. The guy is Emiliano, the letter writer, and a local hire at the small embassy here. These are my angels, here to send me off.

I suppose I'm not very pretty anymore – rope marks on my neck, my face colorless as gravity has taken my blood south. But my hair still looks good. A cherub's curls, someone once said. I wonder if it's true that dead people's hair continues to grow.

Emiliano asks why I'm still dressed – jeans, my snazzy blue aloha shirt printed with pineapples – and Claire reminds him that *here* the family takes care of the biblical stuff, the washing, anointing, and shrouding. Either the family or the mortuary, she says.

"What mortuary?" Emiliano asks.

"Exactly," Claire says.

Emiliano nods and then tells her about the local minister who offered to bury me -- with full church rites -- on his family land. But Jason's mother wouldn't hear of it.

"She'll regret that decision," Claire says. "She should have taken the offer and flown here for the burial." Claire explains – "an unembalmed body shipped with no refrigeration from here to Hawaii, and on to San Diego is not worth transporting."

"Yes, but the mother is insistent," Emiliano tells her.

"Your boss is an idiot for giving in," Claire says.

"It wasn't Greg," Emiliano says, "it was the Ambassador."

"Figures," Claire says, and adds she suspects that it's probably illegal to ship an unembalmed body.

"I've talked to Mrs. Tovar, his mother," Emiliano says, "and she can be pretty persuasive. She asked if there was a gold chain. There wasn't one when the body got here, right?"

Claire shakes her head. "We got him just the way he is. The cops said they emptied his pockets and left everything in the hotel room. Anyway, a gold chain and a rope on the neck don't mix."

"I know the cops didn't take it," Emiliano says,"

they'd be afraid of ghosts."

"Ghosts, my foot, "Claire whispers under her breath.

Meanwhile, me, the corpse, is enjoying listening to my angels.

Claire is absolutely correct. When I arrived at the stateside mortuary, I was unviewable and unfixable. They had never seen such a mess. My unembalmed body was the "shipping arrangements" Emiliano apologized for in his letter. He is truly a sweetheart. He took my mother's mission seriously – to find that damned gold chain. But Claire's wrong about one thing: there are such things as ghosts. I know because I am one.

In that movie M.A.S.H. – not the TV show and, yeah, it has those periods between the letters – there's this guy who pretends to be an angel and in an angel's voice he sings this song about suicide being painless. And then – I can't get over this – I found out some 14-year-old kid wrote those lyrics.

I don't know about it being painless as I was too

drunk to feel anything. I do know it is timeless because I'm both here in the hospital morgue on this so-called island paradise and, at the same time, I'm already in the ground at Christ Memorial Gardens in San Diego.

My mother is not happy about me being buried in a generic, non-denominational cemetery, without a proper Catholic funeral. The head priest at Holy Rosary, the same guy who blesses and sprinkles holy water on the tuna fleet every year, is a hard-liner. She should not have been surprised when he wagged his crooked old finger in her face and lectured her about suicide being a mortal sin. No Catholic burial, no exceptions!

Makes no matter to me where I am, but maybe I'm better off in San Diego. Here there's all that rain. I'd never seen so much rain in all my life. It rained the whole time I was here, two solid weeks, and it totally wore me out. The locals seem to thrive on it – the youngsters run out and play in it while the adults just wait it out or use a banana leaf for an umbrella. I know that if I were in the ground here, I'd feel like I was constantly dying over and over again, only drowning.

In the water, you get eaten by the fishes. Is that better than getting eaten by worms and maggots? What about cremation? I've heard that bodies sit up on the slab while they're being fried, rather like bacon curling. Anyway, I'm worm food at Christ Memorial Gardens.

All fishermen must think long and hard about drowning, but I've never heard them talk about it. I've thought about dying that way because that's how my dad died. We never got his body back. I guess that's why my mother had been so insistent on getting me back.

Some say drowning is not so bad, but I find that hard to believe. I remember as a kid getting water up my nose when I was learning to swim, and it hurt like hell. Hanging is okay, as long as you don't do it wrong and end up strangling yourself. For me, it was over in a snap. And, as I said, I was too drunk to feel anything.

Did you notice the letter Emiliano sent my mother was not on official US State Department stationery? His little investigation of my death was totally unofficial. He knew he was coloring outside the lines, telling her a whole lot more than necessary. She had already received the official letter, all properly written, saying your son died and we're damned sorry it happened here, and here is his suicide note.

The cops who took me down put the rope and all the stuff from my pockets inside the hotel room. When Greg Landau, the deputy-whatever of the US Embassy, came to pack me out, he brought Emiliano along to help. I got to watch them play with the rope, trying to make a lasso, trying to twirl it like in an old cowboy movie. Acting like a couple of comics. I'm surprised the rope held me. A skimpy thing, better for tying up a dog. But it was all I could find.

I left umpteen suicide notes and they picked out the most legible one, destroyed the rest. I thought leaving a note for my mother was the best way, that I was doing her a favor by not waiting until I got home. In truth, I was afraid the Coronado Bridge wasn't tall enough to serve my purpose, that I'd easily survive the jump and hanging myself from it would be too complicated.

It was Emiliano's idea to leave out the pair of pink nylon panties they found – size extra-large. There was a brief argument over this, the deputy-whatever saying regulations require that *everything* has to be packed and shipped to next of kin. Then another of their comedy routines – were the panties left behind by some huge-bottomed girl or were they mine and I liked the *slicky* feel of them?

The most fun I had here was after I was dead – traipsing around with Emiliano when he made the rounds of all the bars during his "unofficial" investigation. I wrapped my arms around his neck, my chin resting on his shoulder, and draped myself down his back. So sweet, like being a ghostly *lei.*

Emiliano's not a bar hound. He's got a pretty wife and a couple of little kids. So, he made the rounds during the day and not at night when he might have been mistaken for someone trying to pick up a bar girl. *Wanteds,* they're called here. Is it because they want to be wanted? That's the impression I got from Rita and her friends.

Lukas was one of the many locals I met by

sitting next to him on a bar stool. That place was not as low-down as others. In fact, the clientele was an older crowd, mostly expats, politicians, government workers, business owners. A cheery place, but one can't sit in one place all night. Plus, it didn't tolerate true drunks and that was what I was. The bartender would cut you off if you slurred or didn't sit up straight.

I only liked being in the bars. Otherwise, there was the constant rain and nothing to do, nowhere to go. What should have been a beautiful green island was nothing but a gray wall of rain. Lots of times the wipers of the rental car couldn't keep up and it was like a gray sheet had been hung across the windshield in front of me. I drove as slow as possible and hung my head out the side window, fearing running off the road or, worse, running over someone, some kid. The main road near my hotel passed through one particular neighborhood where the kids came out to play in the rain, a small gang of them, filling the street, literally dancing and turning cartwheels.

The bar down at the docks is pretty sleazy, but

that night the regular bartender was off, and his son was tending. What a beauty. The *wanteds* I met, Rita and her friends, were dead-eyed. But this lovely – you should have seen the sparkle in his eyes. I'd never met anyone so alive. When I gave him the gold chain, when I hooked the clasp at the back of his neck, he gave me a kiss.

So, what happens: I fall in love and then I hang myself. When you're that liquored up and you've already decided to do something stupid, nothing can change your mind.

I hated working the boats, probably because I was detoxing the whole time we were at sea. Then we returned to port and I'd immediately start back drinking. I couldn't seem to break the loop.

I come from a family of Portuguese fishermen, both sides, many generations. Now my mother knows I hated being one, and because of me being a suicide, she had to switch churches, from Holy Rosary to Saint Agnes, farther down the Point Loma peninsula, in the hope no one will recognize her.

I'm dead so I should have no regrets, right? But

I can't let go of that M.A.S.H. song: *through early morning rain I see the life that was withheld from me, and now I join eternity...* Nope, not the real lyrics. I can't remember those. But, yes, I'm off to join that vast river of departed souls, that all-loving, all-joyous, all-glorious congregation. And as soon as I get there, I'll beg for a do-over. Maybe they'll let me come back here, to this island, and I can be a kid who loves to play in the rain.

HELEN

The creaking sound alerts me to the opening of the Embassy's main door. The security guard peeks around the corner and I give him a wink. He grins, satisfied that I'm at the reception desk, then opens the door wide. I welcome an American couple with a small child. Once in, the toddler wiggles out of his mother's arms and makes his escape, running pell-mell down the long hallway toward the office of the ambassador who is, as usual, off-island. The mother scampers after the child, calling: "Hayden! Hayden!" Meanwhile the father approaches the reception desk and asks for Greg, Greg Landau being the deputy chief.

Looking up, I tell him Mr. Landau has gone to Kosrae, and add that he's expected back Thursday, on the afternoon flight.

The doctor's blue-green eyes brighten. "Oh, Helen," he says. "We met at the hospital. Salvador's your uncle, right? Great guy."

I nod. "Yes, a great guy." But I don't add that he's not really my uncle. Instead, I reach down, unlock the bottom desk drawer to retrieve the doctor's renewed passport. I slide it across the desk toward him, then offer him my pen and the receipt for his signature.

I ask if he would like to see Emiliano Welter?

He shakes his head and signs the form. He examines the pen before handing it back. "It's an honest to god fountain pen," he says, "a real antique."

I tell him it was my grandfather's, and that I special order ink for it at the local stationery store.

When his wife returns with the squirming boy in her arms, Dr. Olson starts to introduce us, but she interrupts him. Turning to me she says, "Sylvia, just Sylvia." She tries to offer me her hand, but both are very much needed to control the child. We both laugh.

"And who is this young man," I ask?

"This," the doctor says, "is William Hayden Olson."

The child is obviously part local and part Anglo. What's called *hapa haole* in Hawaii. Of course, I had already heard the story of how the Olsons acquired the child. There are no secrets on a small island. But for some reason, maybe just the oddity of the Olsons calling the child by his middle name, I ask if Hayden is a family name.

The couple exchange a look, and Sylvia tells me the boy's birth mother requested it. She thinks it might be the name of the child's father, although in the court proceedings for the adoption the mother claimed she didn't know the father's name, only that he....

Dr. Olson interrupts by taking the child from her. She shrugs and gives me a raised eyebrow.

"Well, William Hayden Olson," I say, looking up at the child, "I am very pleased to meet you." To my smile, he returns a blank, wide-eyed stare, not unexpected from someone his age.

I freeze my smile until the couple and their acquired child have left the building, and then spend the next few minutes fretting over the child's fate, imagining different scenarios, finally settling on a happy one: a loving household, good American schools, and the boy following his adoptive father's footsteps into a respected medical career.

I know my "uncle" Salvador has the highest respect for Dr. Olson, and Salvador has a pretty good bullshit detector.

Still, the exchange with the Olson family

has left me in a crappy mood. I call and cancel lunch with Serlina, my best friend from high school. When I left for school, Serlina stayed and married a man who became a rising star in local government. I envy Serlina, not for her fancy husband, but that she knows both her parents, all her grandparents, and who her great-grandparents were.

Like Hayden, I am also *hapa haole.* I know little about my native side which was mixed: local and Japanese. My mother's Japanese father was colonist, an engineer in charge of the hydroelectric plant. His first wife was also Japanese, and died not long after her only child, my Uncle Shige was born. My grandfather then took a local wife, an orphan named Armina who had been living in his household as a ward of his cook and gardener. My grandmother's parents were a local woman and an earlier Japanese colonist who had both died when their daughter was still an infant. At the end of WWII, my Japanese grandfather was repatriated, but left without my grandmother, Armina and her infant daughter, my mother. Trying to keep all this straight in my head, makes me dizzy.

Helen, my exceedingly *haole* given name, puzzles me. My mother always shrugs when questioned. It's just a name, she says, a name she liked.

From my grandmother, Armina, I learned my mother's real given name was Mariko, but at the end of the war, my grandmother decided a less Japanese sounding name would be better. So, my mother was renamed Maria, for the Christian Virgin Mary. My grandmother may have realized later that a Japanese name would not have been a problem as so many islanders were part Japanese after twenty years of colonialism. But by then my mother was well into her grammar school years and quite settled with her new name. Still, all through my growing up years and forever, I only ever heard my grandmother call my mother, Mari-chan.

Skipping my usual lunch hour, I manage to appear busy with small tasks until late afternoon when I tell Emiliano I need the rest of the day off. Family matters, I tell him. The U.S. Embassy here operates in a very relaxed manner, making a show of strict office protocol only when the Ambassador is on-island, which is a rarity. Emiliano has told me the Ambassador deplaned with a bag of golf clubs slung over his shoulder and the crowd at the terminal laughed at him. The island has no golf course, just a private 3-hole course to which he's never been invited. So much for studying the country to which one has been appointed.

There are often times when Emiliano, a local hire, is the highest-ranking staff member on-island to meet and greet. He once met with two Tahitian diplomats, once with a senior statesman from a neighboring island, once with a U.S. senator, and has met fairly often with junketing US government personnel from various departments.

With Emiliano's blessing I set off downhill, a fifteen to twenty-minute walk, to my mother's place. I was determined to confront her with what I learned at my grandmother's bedside. A little over a year ago, I had been called away from a class and given a message my grandmother was extremely ill and I must return home immediately. There was a flight that day and I was told to pack and go directly to the airport where a ticket would be waiting.

After the usual nine-hour flight from Hawaii, my stepfather Valerio met me at the terminal.

"Is she dying," I asked?

He shrugged. "You know how dramatic Armina can be," he said, "but your mother is worried."

At home, I went directly to my grandmother's room. From the doorway, I could see her, tiny and frail, smothered in blankets and propped on pillows. I tapped on the doorframe, announced myself, then bowed and formally greeted her.

"Come," my grandmother said, in a weak

voice. She pulled an arm from beneath the blankets and motioned to me. "Come here. Find the pillow," she pointed behind her, though she didn't say which pillow. When she leaned forward, I extracted one. "Yes," she said, "that one," and she stroked her hand across the cover which must have once been a fashionable kimono.

"Look inside," she told me, "but not now." "Something for you and something for Shige," she said, naming my Japanese uncle. "Promise you will put this in his hands."

"Yes, grandmother, I promise."

"He came," she said.

I nodded. "Yes, I know."

My grandmother wagged her head from side to side. "I was so afraid," she whispered. "I told him to come but I was too afraid to tell him."

I was puzzled as I had never known my grandmother to be afraid of anything.

She beckoned to me to come closer as if for an embrace, then, reaching up she brought my ear to her mouth and whispered a name. She whispered it twice, before relaxing back on the remaining pillows.

I repeated the name.

"Your father," she said. "American government." Her last words to me as she patted the pillow were: "No more secrets. Shige will tell you."

I held her hand until she fell asleep. There was a small smile on her face, a smile of peace and satisfaction.

I spent most of that week sitting by her bed, holding her hand. I then returned to school without waiting for the end. On the flight back, during those endless hours of gazing at sea and sky and clouds, I was flooded with memories, especially of my childhood years after my mother had left for Hawaii when my grandmother and I lived alone in the house that served as a *ryokan* or small hotel. It had been the least expensive accommodation on island and most of our guests were arriving or departing Peace Corps, or world travelers with just a backpack as luggage. But my grandmother giving me the name of my father preoccupied me. Had my mother met him at my grandmother's ryokan or at some local bar during her during her wild days?

I was relieved when the pillow passed through customs with no question. Not until I returned to my dorm room, did I remove the cushion's outer cover and then a thick layer of *kapok.* Inside I found an old-fashioned fountain pen and a notebook filled with Japanese script. I did not read Japanese. I assumed the pen was for me, and that I was to give the notebook to my uncle.

When I was about twelve Uncle Shige came to visit. At dinner he told us about a notebook he found in his late father's desk and he began to tell us what was in the notebook when my grandmother threw a fit, saying it was all lies, that the notebook was completely fabricated.

I considered asking one of my teachers to

translate it. I then thought it better to honor my promise to give it directly to my uncle.

When the news came of my grandmother's death, I did not return home for the funeral and my mother did not insist. Armina did not have any local family, so the funeral was low key. I knew it was better to have visited when she was still alive.

There was also the economic factor, the expense of airfare. I rarely returned home during school breaks, but instead spent the time alone in the dorm. I had not gotten close to my schoolmates, many of whom had families locally, and declined the few invitations I did receive to spend breaks with their families. Staying on campus gave me extra time for library research. Most of my classmates in the Pacific Studies program had strong backgrounds in their own island cultures, and I did not.

A few of my grammar school teachers told stories of island history and local myths, but all in all, I knew so little. The children's songs I learned from my grandmother were all in Japanese.

Understandable, I reasoned, as my grandmother was half-Japanese and had been raised in a Japanese island household. My grandmother and I always spoke Japanese with each other, as she was far from fluent in the native language, and her English was very scanty. I was often needed to act as her translator during my childhood for both English and the local language. English was taught in school while our native tongue was the language of the playground.

At the end of my final year of college, I graduated with honors, and upon my return to the island, my stepfather Valerio finessed a job for me as a receptionist at the newly opened U.S. Embassy.

Once settled in, I asked Emiliano Welter, who was my immediate supervisor, if he could find out anything about an American government official who had been on-island in the early to mid-1960s, and I gave him the name my grandmother told me. I told him the man was my father. It did not take Emiliano long to discover the man had been quite an important official but had since retired from government work.

My rapport with Emiliano had been immediate, but conflicted, at least on my side. Although he felt like a brother, I was also attracted to him. I admired how he conducted his life. He and his wife had a small place in town and their kids went to school here, but they spent every weekend with extended family in the country. He would fish with the men while she cooked with the women and looked after the children. In the country, they lived the island culture.

In the late afternoon, my mother's restaurant is quiet. When I arrive, Lena is ringing out the register and sorting the money. My mother is at a far table, bending over an accounts ledger. I ask Lena if the kitchen can make a couple of fish tacos, my current favorite among the menu items. Tacking back through the roomful of tables with their chairs perched upside down on top, I seat myself across from my mother. She does not look up but merely raises an eyebrow in greeting while continuing to sort through a pile of small pieces of paper and notating in the ledger.

When Lena brings my plate, and I eat.

Finally, my mother closes the ledger. "Well?" she asks.

"Good," I mumble with my mouth full. I swallow. "They're always good," I say. When I finish, I push the plate aside, wipe my fingers clean on a napkin and tell her: "I'm going to Japan."

She rolls her eyes and brushes away the idea as if swatting at a fly.

"It's a done deal," I tell her. "I've saved for the airfare and Uncle Shige is expecting me."

"You don't even know him," my mother replies.

I counter: "he's your own brother and my uncle."

"Half-brother, half-uncle," my mother corrects me.

I fake a laugh. "Like my *step*-father and my

half-sister?"

My mother jerks back as if from a physical blow.

"So, half-this and half-that," I say, waving a hand back and forth, "and me *hapa haole*. Whatever. In a month I am going to Japan to visit your *half*-brother and his wife."

"No," my mother says. "You need to stay here. For now, you're only a receptionist, but you're smart and will move up. It's a good job and you should be grateful to Valerio."

"I am grateful," I say, "but I don't want to spend my life working for the Americans." I take a deep breath. "Someday I would like to be an ambassador for our own country."

"But, but ...," my mother sputters.

"I'm not talking about tomorrow," I tell her. "But someday."

She narrows her eyes and asks who I've told about my plans.

I tick them off on my fingers: Claire, Uncle Salvador, Emiliano.

My mother throws her arms in the air: "you tell all of them before telling me, your own mother!"

"I needed their advice," I say, "and Claire especially has never set me wrong."

"And I have," my mother asks?

"Sometimes," I whisper with my head lowered, "talking to you has been difficult."

She answers, also in a whisper, "I'm sorry you felt you could not come to me."

"Plus," I say, looking up, "I would like to see Japan. The other part of our heritage."

She shrugs. "That, I suppose, is reasonable."

"And I need to improve my Japanese language skills," I tell her.

She asks how long I intend to be away.

"My ticket is open-ended, but probably only a few months, six at the most."

She nods. "As long as you come back to us," she says, reaching her hands across the table.

I meet her hands with mine. "Do I have your blessing," I ask?

"You do," she answers.

I pause, draw a deep breath, and say in a rush: "When I came to see grandmother before she died, she told me the name of my father."

My mother is stunned, totally speechless.

I have never seen her at a loss for words. I lean forward: "Do you remember his name?" I ask.

She looks to the ceiling and shakes her head. Looking back at me she says, he left, and I never heard from him again. She slumps back in her chair. After a long silence, she says: "he was tall and handsome, a gentle lover, older but not old. It was many years later that I came to understand what had really happened, how he had been under the spell of this place." She spreads her arms. "Our island is exotic to these gentlemen from Washington. He probably thought he was on *Bali Ha'i*."

"*Bali Ha'i?*"

My mother explains. *Bali Ha'i* was a fictional island in the movie South Pacific. She had seen it on late night TV when she lived in Hawaii.

"It was then," she says, "that I realized I must have been the perfect island girl for him, the girl of his dreams, bright but uneducated, and in my youth," she adds, "I was a beauty. He may have even wished he could have whisked me home with him. But of course, his family would never have accepted me. So, he left, and I never saw him again."

"How did grandmother deal with it? With you being pregnant?" I ask.

"Not a scandal here, as you know. And Salvador smoothed things over. He and I had once been sweethearts and were still good friends. He claimed the child I was having was his, but when you were born, one look and it was obvious he could not have been your father. So, he became your promise uncle, your godfather. I suspect he even made it official by taking you to the Catholic priest and having you baptized."

I gasp! "I've been baptized!" We both laugh into our hands.

At the airport, I recognize my Uncle Shige, not difficult after our years of exchanging photos and brief letters. We bow politely. "Welcome, Helen," he says.

I lean around him, looking to one side and then the other. "Where is your wife?" I ask.

He shakes his head. "I don't have one," he answers, almost in a whisper. "I feared your parents would not allow you to come if I did not have a wife. Isn't a wife a very important commodity?"

I raise my hands to cover my mouth, then burst out laughing.

Shige, too, covers his mouth. Now we are both laughing.

Once we gain control ourselves, we pick up my bag and depart by train for Tokyo. During the trip, I attempt to initiate small talk. He responds to my remarks on the scenery or the weather with grunts, or he answers with *hai, hai* while nodding his head.

Finally, I get a real response when I tell him

I'm impressed he can pronounce my name properly. "You know," I say, "that damned 'L'. I've often wished my name were Erin. I was going to tell you to call me that if it were easier."

"I had a good teacher," he says, finally relaxing, and he begins to talk. He tells me his housekeeper is away visiting her sister and for at least a day, maybe two, we will be alone in the house. "Rose always visits her sister this time of year," he tells me. "She has no other family as her mother was disinherited when she married a foreigner."

"A foreigner?"

"Yes, a German diplomat. He was recalled before the war and they never heard from him again. Rose assumes he died during the war and her mother, who had heart problems, died before the end of the war."

"So, Rose taught you English?"

"Yes. Rose speaks Japanese, German, English, and some French. She studied literature at university, and she loves to read. The storeroom closet is full of her books."

"A rather extraordinary person for a housekeeper," I comment, and my uncle nods his agreement.

When the train pulls into the busy Tokyo station, we change to another train. Only a short while later, he indicates the station just announced is ours. When we exit the station, he leads me down a market street, pulling my suitcase, the wheels bumping across the uneven pavement. I carry my backpack slung across one shoulder and move up to walk beside him whenever the crowd thins.

The market is like nothing I have ever seen. A loud *pachinko* parlor announces itself on one side, the fish shop on the other side displays large slabs of very dark red meat. "Whale meat," Shige tells me when I ask. I swing my head back and forth, from one side of the street to the other: a tiny tofu factory, then ladies' wear, a stationery shop, pottery and tableware, mechanical toys, candy shops, vegetable shops, places that appear to be neighborhood bars, and others selling noodles, and another stall specializing in gourmet insects such as fried wasps and grasshoppers.

For me, the market street's aromas are exotic and delightful. Shige notes my raised nose, sniffing when we pass a small restaurant. He checks his watch and tells me it's almost time for supper to be delivered. "Every night," he says, "we have noodles for the evening meal. Our breakfasts are simple: fruit and coffee, toast if you would like, rice or oat porridge, if that suits you. There is always something substantial for the mid-day meal, but you must say if you want something different."

"Come," he says, as he veers off into a side street. After a turn or two, he stops in front of a gate. Looking up, I see behind the fence the old-fashioned tiled roof of a two-story house. He opens the gate and I follow him to a door which he unlocks and slides open.

The floor of the entry is covered in dark slate pavers. Shige indicates to the right a cabinet where outside shoes are stored. Two pairs of soft house slippers have been set out on the platform above, apparently waiting for us. I whisper that I need to use a toilet.

"The Japanese one is to your right," Shige says, "or I can take you back to the western one." I tell him the Japanese one is fine, and when I return, he is waiting at the foot of the stairs, my rolling suitcase and my backpack on the floor beside him. He points. "Your room is up," he says, "but first let me show you the rest of the house."

He turns to the left side of the foyer and opens a western-style door. "My room," he tells me. The room is large with high ceilings, the walls painted a cream color, and pale contemporary carpeting. French doors in the far wall appear to open to a garden. Glass fronted cabinets are arrayed on one side, and a large multi-mullioned window on the other with a modern sofa below it. He points: "there's my father's desk where I found the notebook and the ledger that led me to find your mother and Armina. The sofa opens out into my bed," he explains. "When my father was alive the room was our western style living room, but Rose and I really have no use for such a specialized room, so I moved down here from upstairs."

Shige leads me back across the foyer to a long hallway on the right. After the door to the Japanese toilet, there are sliding doors painted with yellow chrysanthemums. "Rose's old room," he says, "now used as a storeroom. I expect someday it will be converted into a maid's room, but for now, a maid comes in three days a week." We continue down the hallway. He slides open a panel with glass panes in the upper part. He flips a switch, illuminating the kitchen. "If we want to cook before Rose returns," he tells me.

"I'm not much of a cook," I say. "Are you?"

He shakes his head. "I always go out when Rose is gone. Except for morning coffee and evening noodles."

I linger as if drawn to this room. Same as the entry, the kitchen is down a level and has the same dark slate floor. The room is not too big, not too small, on one side is a row of gas burners beside a deep sink, on the other side a large refrigerator and glass-fronted cabinets filled with tableware. In the middle is an island, and on the outside wall, a sliding door with glass upper panes that mimic the other door.

Shige looks at his watch. "The noodle fellow will let himself in," he tells me. "Soon, we'll find our supper waiting. Come," he says, and I follow.

At the end of the hallway, he slides open yet another door. A small room with a large mirror above a sink, a countertop with one side crowded with tins of talc, jars of cream, and a stack of hand towels, the other side bare. Along the inside wall are hooks with towels and bathrobes.

Shige steps into the room and slides open an interior door on the right. I'm tall enough to easily look over his shoulder, into a tiled room with a deep wooden tub set into a waist-high counter along the back wall. A hand-held shower gizmo protrudes from the nearer wall, a low stool below it.

"More," he says, and turns me back into the hallway. He points to another door on the right but does not open it. "Western-style toilet," he says. Then on to a large *tatami*-matted room, bare except for a low table with cushions. "Rose's room," he says. Without being told, I understand the room must have once been my grandfather's. On one side are floor to ceiling windows that open to the garden.

"Come," he says and turns down yet another long hallway. On the right, a wall of sliding doors with floor to ceiling glass panels open into a garden. I gaze out on a wide expanse of grass with a wide band of shrubs and small trees on the periphery hiding the fence line.

"Here," Shige says, and I turn to watch him slide open a set of *shoji* screens, exposing two stately rooms, both *tatami*-matted, a low table with cushions in one room, the farther room bare. I notice the room's fancy sliding screens along two walls, more yellow and gold chrysanthemum. I assume they hide deep storage cabinets.

Shige points directly across to the far side of the first room. "The kitchen is there," he explains, "behind that sliding door."

I realize that the hallways of the house form a rectangle with these two rooms as islands in the middle and that around the next corner is the foyer where we started.

Shige carries my suitcase up the steep narrow staircase and shows me where to stow my things, then pulls a *futon* and bedding from a closet and spreads them out. "They were aired yesterday," he tells me.

I note the view out the window, again floor to ceiling glass panels, down into the garden. It's the most beautiful room I've ever had, and it's all mine. At home, I share with my sister and at school with an assigned roommate.

Returning downstairs, we find noodles waiting in the kitchen. He gets two cold beers and glasses, then shows me where the spoons and chopsticks are kept. I carry one tray and he the other across the hall where we sit across the low table from each other.

We dig in. He slurps, and I mimic him. "Wonderful," I say. He smiles.

When we finish, I tell him to wait. I skip up the stairs to my new room and retrieve the notebook my grandmother had entrusted me to deliver directly into my uncle's hands.

Back downstairs, I push the notebook across the table toward him. It is not a surprise as I had written to him months ago telling him I was bringing it, but he seems oddly emotional and thanks me effusively.

The next morning, over coffee and papaya, Shige tells me he read the notebook.

"The whole thing? "

He nods.

"And?"

"It's a treasure," he says.

"Tell me," I say.

He shakes his head. "Best to go at this

slowly," he says. "You need to start with the first notebook, the one I found in my father's desk. I've already talked to Rose and she agrees the notebooks will be excellent material for you to translate. She is looking forward to this as she found the first notebook so intriguing."

"Rose will be my teacher? She doesn't mind?"

Shige shakes his head. "Both notebooks are fascinating. And you two will get along ... famously? Is that right?"

I nod. "Famously," I echo. "But tell me, why does your housekeeper have the best room in the house?"

"It's complicated," he answers.

I laugh. "What isn't," I say.

Shige then explains the house actually belongs to Rose. His father, my grandfather, only leased it all those years ago, and a condition of the lease was that Rose would be employed as housekeeper, would live on-site, and be paid wages. In other words, Rose is Shige's landlord.

I lift my eyebrows and tilt my head, indicating I want more.

He pauses, then lets out a breath with a long sigh. "Listen," he says and begins: "Japan was a defeated country at the end of the war. The citizens had paid dearly, the cities in ruins, and the economy absolutely busted. Even once well-off families found themselves impoverished, without a livelihood, and to survive many offered their homes for lease to foreign nationals, most of whom were the higher-ups of the American occupational military, or diplomats from the various embassies. When my father, your grandfather, was repatriated he learned all his immediate family had perished in one of the many Tokyo fire bombings. The family home had been destroyed and all that was left was money in banks."

I interrupt. "What about your mother's family?"

Shige shrugs. "My father never said. There was so much confusion after the war. I don't think he ever looked for them. He was a different man, a sad man. But as an engineer, he was in high demand for rebuilding the war-ravaged city. We did not live lavishly, and he had no expensive vices. I can easily live off what he left, without touching the capital. And Rose," he adds, "has been prudent, living off her housekeeping salary and banking the lease money all those years. How do they say in English: a pretty penny?"

"Yes, a pretty penny."

"In addition, and most importantly, Rose has been a mother to me, my third mother. The real one died when I was too young to remember her. For a time, I was cared for by the cook and the gardener, then I had Armina, and then Rose. The only relative Rose has left is a sister who married well and lives in Kobe."

"Was Rose my grandfather's mistress?"

Shige shrugs. "I don't know," he says, "but they were fond of each other."

"Don't you have to go to work today?" I ask.

He gives me a puzzled look.

"Aren't you a woodworker or some kind of carpenter?"

Shige groans and slaps a hand across his eyes. "Can you handle another lie?" he asks. "First my fake wife and now my fake profession. Do you remember those vitrines in my room?"

"Vitrines?"

"The glass cabinets? They hold my collection of *netsuke*. I make real money buying and selling them. I no longer trade in real ivory as they are a risky investment and illegal in many countries. My *netsuke* are my children, and most are fashioned from precious woods or ivory nuts."

"Your children? "

"Since I have no human children," he says, "I have pets. I specialize in animals: whales, rabbits, owls, monkeys, cats, horses, ducks, dolphins, sheep, turtles, squirrels. Come, I will show you."

I follow him to his room. He opens a cabinet and hands me a tiny rabbit. "It looks and feels like ivory," he tells me, "but is carved from an ivory nut. They grow on your island."

I nod and tell him there are many ivory nut palms growing farther along the peninsula road that goes by my parent's house. In my hand the tiny animal feels so smooth and silky. I can imagine carrying it in a pocket and stroking it constantly as if it were a good luck piece or a Catholic rosary or a set of Middle Eastern worry beads.

I hand it back. "So soothing," I say. "Your children are beautiful."

Our straight-backed postures mimic each other as we sit on the cushions in Rose's room, the low table between us. We're so similar I want to giggle. We both have oriental eyes. My hair is medium brown, shoulder length, with a fringe of bangs. Rose has silver woven through her dark hair which she wears much like an island woman: pulled back in a chignon at the nape and held in place with hair sticks. We are wearing what each of us will learn is practically a uniform for the other:

Rose in a twin set, a longish skirt and thick stockings; me in jeans and a T-shirt or sweatshirt, and barefoot or in socks, depending on the weather.

On my side of the table rests a school tablet and a text for learning and practicing Japanese characters, and on top, my beloved fountain pen. In front of Rose is the notebook. We have agreed to speak English during the lessons, and Japanese at all other times.

"This is not the one you brought;" Rose says, smoothing a hand across the top of the notebook. "This is the earlier one." Then she asks me to tell her what I know about it.

I begin: "when Uncle Shige first visited the island about ten years ago, he told us that after his father's death he found this notebook. We also learned he found a ledger notating money sent to the island for my grandmother, and for my mother's upbringing. Everyone was at the table when he told us: me, my mother, my grandmother, and my mother's husband."

"Your stepfather," Rose says.

"Yes, my stepfather. We were in the middle of dinner when Uncle Shige told us the notebook he found detailed the war years and was written by an unknown woman. Before he could say anything more, my grandmother stood up and angrily threw down her napkin. She said the notebook was a total lie, and she left the table."

I've been staring at the notebook as it looks exactly like the one I brought. I pause and glance up at Rose, who nods for me to continue.

"Even at my age, I could see that everyone was very... very..."

"Embarrassed?" Rose suggests.

"Yes, embarrassed. I remember uncle apologizing for not bringing a photocopy. He told us the original was too precious to risk bringing. We finished the meal, but my parents changed the conversation to such things as the weather and how Uncle Shige was enjoying his stay."

Again, Rose smooths her hand across the top of the notebook. "Shige keeps this locked in a fireproof box. I'm surprised he doesn't keep it in a safety deposit box at the bank. He thinks the notebooks, this one and one you brought should be published, as Japanese colonial history."

"Really? And you have read them both?"

"Yes," Rose says. "I think Shige is correct to want to publish them. But first, please, take a good look at this notebook." She hands it across to me and I open it.

"What do you see?" Rose asks. "Anything familiar?"

I gasp. It appears to have been written with the same pen as the one I brought with me. I stroke my beloved pen. "Could it be," I ask, "that this pen wrote both?"

Rose says, "I want you to think about that, and about how your grandmother came to have the pen that might have written both notebooks. But now to work." She opens the first notebook and begins to read. I translate into English. But at only the second entry, I hold up my hands.

"Stop," I say, "that sounds like my

grandmother's *ryokan*."

Rose raises her eyebrows, encouraging me to continue.

I shrug. "How can it be? Even the name is the same as my grandmother's *ryokan*. We lived there until my mother married my stepfather, when I was about nine years old."

A day or so later, Rose stops the translation. She tells me she knows from Shige about this scene of a man saying goodbye to his son. "The boy is Shige," she says, "and the man is his father, your grandfather."

I give her a quizzical look.

"Yes," she says. "The man was your grandfather and the boy he was saying goodbye to on the day with all the flowers is your Uncle Shige."

"How can that be? How is it this woman knew my grandfather?"

Rose shakes her head. "She did not know

him. She merely records the scene. As we will see later in the notebook, it probably reminded her of her own life, of when her soldier husband went off to war."

I tell Rose that yesterday Shige said I needed to get to know this woman. I thought he meant you. No, he told me, you need to get to know the woman of the notebook. Why should I? I asked. She's a brothel worker. He explained it was a perfectly legal profession at that time, and not likely something a woman would choose for herself. He said her alternatives must have been worse.

"All true," Rose says. "Also, the woman has a name. Would you like to know it?"

I nod, and Rose turns the notebook around. She points to the top of the back page, to what is the front page in Japanese-style books. "Mieko," Rose says. "How about we call her that from now on?"

Shige brought me a low table to use as a

desk upstairs in my room. Seated there, against the windows, I can look down on the garden when I pause to think or feel day dreamy. From up there I can hear faint sounds from below, the maid going about her work, dusting, mopping, etc. Once a week the laundry is sent out and comes back fresh and sweet-smelling. I do the cleaning of my room and the stairs leading to it and bring my laundry down to her.

Mornings, while Rose is out shopping and then preparing the mid-day meal, my task is memorizing and copying Japanese characters. I feel like a First Grader, but I consider Rose a perfect teacher. I'm pleased my study is "in house" and I do not have to adjust to an outside, professional teacher. We settle into the routine of spending every afternoon translating the notebook. "It's like a diary," I say, "but different."

Rose tells me it is similar to a pillow book, a classic Japanese genre that is more a recording of impressions than a Western-style diary. The name comes from where the book would be kept, inside a *takamakura*, the tall hollow pillow that held a woman's complicated coiffure intact while she slept.

I tell her I read Sei Shonagon's Pillow Book in school. "So, like that?" I ask.

Rose wags her head: both yes and no. "Sei's pillow book was written for an audience," she says, "but this," she taps the notebook, "was private. Still, the format is similar: a record of insights and musings. But here, we have something more like a chronicle that follows the dailiness of Mieko's life and the events of the war on the island."

Rose appears pleased with our progress. Sometimes she turns the notebook around and has me attempt to read the characters.

At the end of a recent lesson, I ask Rose where she lived during the war.

"Here," Rose says. "This was my mother's house. My father bought it for her as a proper home for his new bride."

"Same as my mother's husband," I say. "Valerio built the house across the estuary when he married my mother. Shortly thereafter, my grandmother and I went to live with them."

Rose nods for me to continue.

Instead, I tell her that Shige told me she is half German. "Me," I confess, "I had an American father. Shige sometimes calls you Mrs. Takahashi. You had a husband?"

"Yes, a young pilot who was killed early on in the war. When I received the news I returned here, to my mother's home. There was nothing that held me to his family, as we had no children. Rather like Mieko in the notebook when her husband was killed. The difference was I had a mother who welcomed me back, and my family were not poor farmers. Mieko feared she would be a burden to her family, so she agreed to be sold to traders who then sold her into a Tokyo brothel. Sorry if I am getting ahead of the notebook."

I shake my head.

She then asks me about my American

father. I give her a brief version, and add that in our culture a child born out of wedlock is not rare and that no one is compelled to wear a red A. "In fact," I say, "many island women demand to be given their first grandchild to raise."

"A sensible culture," Rose remarks.

The household's daily lunch menu is usually fish or seafood with rice, similar to what I ate growing up, but Rose serves the meal artistically on small plates, along with a pickled salad. Sometimes she makes cutlets, like miniature wiener schnitzel, with potatoes and a red cabbage salad. I suspect it might be comfort food from her own childhood.

One day she asks if I would like to cook something, anything? I laugh and tell her: "even though my mother is an excellent cook, I can't cook at all."

"Shige told me about the dinner your mother prepared," Rose says. "He went on and on about it. I understand she is a professional chef?"

"Yes. She has a restaurant, but it is only a lunch place. She is capable of much more, but with a lunchroom, her hours are shorter, and since her customers are mainly government workers, she doesn't open on weekends."

"Your grandmother taught her to cook? "

"Maybe. My grandmother did operate a *ryokan*, but she only served meals when asked. My mother told me that when she was small my grandmother worked as a maid for American missionaries. From them, she may have learned a bit of English and a bit about American cooking. Then, about the time my mother started school, the missionary family left. Now that you have told me more about the ledger and the money sent via the head of one of the Belgian families, I think my grandmother accepted only occasional visitors, more in the late 1960s and early 1970s when American Peace Corps came looking for a cheap place to stay. They would come to town for an R&R from their countryside postings."

I continue: "when I was three or so, my mother went off to a special school for Micronesians set up on the Big Island in Hawaii. The first two years were formal schooling, business administration, she then she moved to Honolulu and worked as kitchen prep or sous chef at various fancy restaurants. During that time, it was just my grandmother and me and a maid who mostly came to do the market shopping." I pause. "When I think about it," I add, "my grandmother was pretty much a recluse. She certainly did not go to church like my friends' mothers and grandmothers."

"Shige told me you acted as his interpreter on his first visit to the island. "

"Yes. My grandmother and I always spoke Japanese. My mother speaks some Japanese but is not fluent. May I tell you? Trying to translate the notebook makes me nervous, yet when I relax, the narrative seems quite understandable. She writes simply."

"She?" Rose says, with a wink.

"Mieko," I answer. "Mieko wrote simply."

"Yes," Rose says. "Her education was fairly basic, but sound. All Japanese children were educated, both girls and boys. The government followed the wisdom of former Emperor Meiji's desire for an educated population."

I tell her the colonial Japanese also educated the islanders, at least for a few years, and students who showed promise were given more. I also tell her I suspect the main reason my grandmother wanted to move to the district center was for my mother's schooling. I shrug. "Just what I suspect," I say.

The maid's days off are weekends, Tuesdays and Thursdays, and on those mornings if Shige is not here and Rose is out shopping, and I find myself alone in the house for an hour or two, I exploit it. Socks on my feet, with Walkman and earphones, I crank up the music. I brought a small handful of my favorite cassettes: Cyndi Lauper,

Tina Turner, The Police, Michael Jackson. I crank up the Walkman and I dance and twirl and slide down the hallways, being careful to not crash into the walls or the *shoji* screens. It feels like being in a roller rink, down one hallway, then another, around and around. Occasionally, I put on the exotic soundtrack from that movie I loved, *A Year of Living Dangerously*, and prance around the hallways to that. It was that movie that first gave me the idea of the foreign service as a career. I was seduced by the movie's exotic location, having drinks at poolside, and whatshisname being so damn handsome. But my mother's confession about my father being seduced by a Hollywood movie has me seriously reconsidering.

When I hear Rose returning from shopping, I hurry to the kitchen to help her put the groceries away. "I hardly ever see uncle anymore," I tell her.

"He's a very private person," she answers. "I suspect he told your family he did woodworking or was a carpenter."

"Yes, that's what he told us. My stepfather was very interested in supplying Shige with exotic woods. But Shige has admitted to me he doesn't do woodworking, He collects *netsuke*."

Rose nods. "I'm pleased he told you himself. He has a very successful business buying and selling those small objects. The men who come, both buyers and sellers, use the garden door to his room so as to not disturb the household. These are not people you should meet," she adds. "They are very rich, and many are very odd, very eccentric. Shige is wise to keep you well away. You are beautiful and an innocent. Those men would gobble you up."

I'm unsure how to respond. "But Shige ..," I say.

"No, not Shige," Rose answers. "But don't ask any more."

Leaves are turning, there's a chill in the air, and mornings I've begun to layer my clothing: T-shirt, then a sweatshirt, and a sweater. Rose notices and says we need to make a shopping list for winter clothing.

I tell her I have some money, and she tells me Shige will outfit me for the winter. "Also," she says, "let's try for something different on the menu today. Hamburgers? Would you like a hamburger?"

"I would love that. Is it possible?"

Rose nods. "Shige, too, loves hamburgers. And maybe you and I should go to the cinema once in a while. How does that sound? A matinee now and then?" It is then that I realize Rose must have had a full life before I arrived, and she herself needs more entertainment.

The next day, Rose stops her reading of the notebook and asks if I believe what my grandmother said that the notebook is false, a fabrication.

I shake my head and say that Mieko wrote about a man in Tokyo who had given her a pen that seems the same as mine. "Of course," I say, "it is not the only pen like this in the world, but did it ever belong to my grandfather? My grandmother never expressly said it was his. I assumed." I sit back and shake my head. "I'm so confused," I whisper.

"I understand," Rose says. "I truly do."

Early that evening I finally give in and take a hot bath. Since my arrival, I have taken only shower baths. Now, with the weather changing, I dare the hot, hot water of the wooden tub. On weekends and the maid's days off I have taken on the task of laying the wood in the firebox in the late afternoons and starting the fire. A chore I enjoy.

I am hoping the water will not be so hot earlier in the evening before the noodles arrive. First, I take the required shower, then into the tub. I lift one leg, dip a foot in, and quickly yank it out. Then put it back and slowly let the leg slide in, up to the knee. I maneuver my bottom up on to the wide ledge, then raise the other leg, dip that foot in, and slowly let my leg sink until my knee is submerged. I raise both legs and observe their lobster redness. People don't die from this, I tell myself. I put my legs back, and slowly let my thighs, inch by inch, slide into the scalding water, until my feet hit the wooden slats at the bottom of the tub. Again, I tell myself, people don't die from this, as I sink into a squat, the water up to my armpits, then over my shoulders, until my butt is resting on a submerged stool. I regret having postponed this for so long and will probably be in love with hot, hot baths for the rest of my life.

A day later, Rose takes me shopping. We ride the train to a large department store, and with Rose as my coach, I select long underwear, two pairs of corduroy trousers, three turtleneck pullovers, and a heavy wool cardigan. Then warm boots and thick socks, a parka with a hood, a pair of warm gloves, also a cozy bathrobe, winter house shoes, and a flannel nightgown. Rose pays for it with Shige's credit card. After all, she tells me, you paid your plane fare here and you brought him something invaluable. The other notebook.

Then the notebook explodes. First, a mention of the engineer, my grandfather, coming to visit the governor general at the brothel where he has now taken up residence. Then only a page or so later the governor general's young corporal is sent to the engineer's house on the river for garden fruits and vegetables. There he sees a young woman who he believes is the engineer's wife and she appears to be expecting a child.

I clap my hand over my mouth and whisper through it: "she must have been my grandmother! And child she expected was my mother!"

"Wait," Rose says. "We are so close to the end of this notebook. Shall we finish it?"

I nod. She reads and I translate, sentence by sentence.

The bombing begins. The ones at the Ifumi, Mieko, Mrs. Okata, the governor general and his corporal are packing to go to the engineer's house on the river, my grandfather's house.

"Did they arrive," I ask? "My grandmother

said they were never there."

Rose closes the notebook. "The answer is in the second notebook, the one you brought to us."

"When can we start that one?"

"Perhaps we should take a break?" She suggests we have a small celebration for reaching the end of the first notebook. "What would you like to do?"

I tell her I would like to go out to lunch to the Vietnamese place Shige took me the day after my arrival, before her return from visiting her sister. "It was a tiny place," I say. "The *bahn mi* rolls were much lighter and crisper than any I ever had in Hawaii."

"Ah," Rose says. "Then they were not regular French baguettes but were made with rice flour. That makes them light and crispy-crusted. Then tomorrow we shall go there." She also reminds me that the holiday season is upon us. "You know our kitchen does not have an oven, so a turkey is out of the question. We could go out to one of the hotels that cater to Westerners for a traditional Christmas dinner. Do you want a Yule tree?"

I shrug. "Maybe we could just hang some fairy lights."

"Like the ones in the notebook," Rose says, "the ones on the rooftop of the department store that Mieko wrote about."

"I know that building," I say, "or what's left of it. Now it's a government machine shop."

"Strings of sparkling lights are a good idea," Rose says. "We can hang them up near the ceiling in the two formal rooms."

After Christmas when Rose and I resume our study of the second notebook, it is obvious the people from the brothel arrived safely. We then concentrate on Santa and Gustof who appear frequently in the second notebook. Rose and I discuss at length who they were and what part they played in the life of my grandmother. I remind her my mother said that as a child she called them auntie and uncle, but that did not mean they were actually related. "Armina's name is an islander name," I add, "whereas Santa and Gustof sound Christian and German-influenced."

Rose nods in agreement.

Then, less than a month later, near the end of translating the second notebook, I have to remind myself: nothing is simple. I am stunned by the description of the death by suicide of my grandmother Armina. I look at Rose and say: "the grandmother who raised me was someone else entirely."

"Did you suspect?" Rose asks.

I shake my head. "I should have," I say. "Especially when it appeared the notebooks were written with the same pen, the same pen my grandmother gave me. Even the character strokes," I say, "the equivalent of handwriting style, were the same."

I sit back on my heels. "My grandmother I knew was Mieko, not Armina."

We both sit through a long silence. She

watches me as I ingest the truth. Then she asks if, or how, I will tell my mother.

I lean my head to the side. "I have to think about that," I answer. "I never told my mother about the notebook my grandmother gave me to bring to Uncle Shige. I told her I was coming to Japan only for language study. But, Rose-san, for me, I must say I love knowing who both of my grandmothers were, the one who died and the one who raised me."

Rose nods. "In the notebooks, Mieko gave us a great lesson," she says, "that a family need not be blood, a family can be created out of necessity or circumstance, or even love, as corny as that sounds. When I think back over the notebooks, before Armina died, your grandfather's household at the house on the river was a family. Even the women of the brothel formed a family of sorts. And now, just as Shige has become my son, you have become my granddaughter."

I smile. "Yes, we are family and you are my grandmother."

"The notebooks are remarkable," Rose says. "They're an important piece of Japanese history, but they are also an intimate history. Most early twentieth-century Japanese women writers wrote fiction, often autobiographical, but nonetheless, fiction. Mieko's voice is intimate and uniquely her own."

I nod.

"Then you understand why Shige and I will work to see that the notebooks are published. Before the war, this neighborhood was home to many writers and poets, people I knew back in my university days and who can facilitate publication. Shige and I would prefer a bilingual book," Rose says. "Perhaps a facsimile of the notebook's pages on one side and an English translation on the opposite page. Your help, Helen, would be invaluable. Should you decide to stay on, you could go to university here. Shige and I would be happy to finance everything."

We are both silent. I look out toward the garden. I am still stunned by the news of Armina's suicide and find the plans for publication a bit overwhelming. I tell Rose I don't know what it is I want.

"Think about it," Rose says, "maybe go for a walk. We can discuss it tonight when Shige is with us."

Later, over our noodles and into the night, the three of us talk for hours. We decide nothing, except that the publication must go forward. I tell them that having my mother read the published book might be the best way for me to tell her. That way she can get to know Mieko slowly, as I did.

Those endless hours of long flights, when one is free to think and daydream, are a treasure to me. Hours of absolute quiet and no need to speak to anyone beyond a yes or a no, and always a window seat to allow viewing the endless sky and ocean, nearly falling into a hypnotic trance colored by the palate of blue and white.

I think of Mieko, of how overjoyed she was

to finally go with Gustof to the sea and walk on the reef flats. The way she wrote about being able to view the sky and the ocean almost seemed to be a religious experience. I wonder if experiencing that may have spurred in her a desire to remain on the island. When the Japanese authorities made it clear no Japanese would be allowed to remain is when she chooses to assume Armina's identity.

When my plane sets down for the Guam layover, I call my mother to tell her I'm on my way and to give her my arrival time. She has at her fingertips a list of things she needs me to buy as if she had been waiting for me to call. She tells me she plans to add *saimin* and teriyaki beef on a stick to her menu. She even tells me which shops to go to.

"Get me a supply of wooden sticks," she says, "plus a case of suitable noodles, rice or *soba*, or in a pinch I can use unseasoned *ramen* noodles, and a dozen large boxes of *dashi* or bonito flakes."

"If this is a success," she says, "I can order regular shipments."

I laugh. "Such great news," I tell her. My mother and I do have in common our times of living in Hawaii. With the secret of my father out of the way, she and I can begin to build a trusting relationship, and our mutual love of Hawaiian street food is as good a start as any.

At the appointed time, Valerio meets me at the terminal. On the drive home I tell him: Shige isn't a woodworker or a carpenter. I think he told us what he thought we wanted to hear.

Valerio shrugs. "Are any us who we say we are?"

I reach over and punch him in the shoulder. "You're one of the good guys," I tell him. And then I ask, "can we get a boat?"

He looks over and gives me a puzzled, "Wha'??"

"I want to work with mama at her place," I tell him, "and on weekends go off to the reef islands or nearby atolls. Can we fish? Do you know how to fish?"

Valerio laughs and says it is good to have me home.

Once home I unpack quickly, having left my new winter clothing in the drawers of the large dresser in what is now my upstairs room at Rose and Uncle's home. Then, my first task is to acquire my own post office box. I write to Rose and we begin exchanging letters once or twice a week, our main topic being preparing Mieko's notebooks for print. The plan is still for dual language, as it will make the book suitable as a historical reference for that period in Japanese history and will be a useful text in both Japanese and American universities. Most of Rose's questions have to do with smoothing the English translation, most especially, with island place names and the occasional use of the native language, specifics on island customs, etc.

The second thing, I buy myself a used car

with some leftover savings and a salary advance from my mother. I am working in the restaurant's kitchen, doing prep work, and pitching in when needed out front waitressing or cashiering during the busy lunch hours.

I've decided to take a very early morning class in world history at the community college. The idea came from the day I spent with Rose at the Meiji Museum, the day we went to find the hole in the wall Shige took me to for the great *banh mi*. The museum visit with Rose was different from when I went with my uncle. With Shige, we admired the beauty and artistry of the displays, but with Rose, it was a history lesson. Rose compared the Emperor Meiji to Ataturk and Franklin Roosevelt, two statesmen whose goals were to bring their countries into the light, light with a capital L. I knew a bit about Meiji but very little about Roosevelt and had never heard of Ataturk. I was humbled to realize how limited my education had been, focused as it was on Pacific Studies. Rather like navel-gazing.

After my morning class, I chop cabbage for slaw and do everything else that needs to be done before opening for lunch. Having watched Rose at work in the kitchen, and occasionally going shopping with her, gave me more appreciation for my mother's skills. Then, in the late afternoons, while my mother is balancing the accounts, Loha who is in middle school, and I sit across from each other and do our homework in the quiet, empty dining room.

One afternoon, near the end of the lunch rush, Emiliano Welter and Greg Landau from the U.S. Embassy pay a surprise visit. I leave the kitchen to sit with them. When I see Emiliano had ordered *saimin*, our new menu item, I ask if it reminded him of school days. Since the island does not yet have a four-year college, Emiliano had been schooled in Hawaii, as many of our professional and semi-professional islanders have been.

"Ah," he says, "it was wonderful, took me back to those exotic, student-affordable, taxi-stop meals. Even Greg, here, tried it -- along with the teriyaki sticks."

"Delicious," Greg says, "absolutely delicious."

I do wonder what Greg really thought, and I'm suddenly reminded of the lovely camaraderie the three of us once shared, especially when we indulged in our end of the day gab sessions. We'd gather in Greg's office and raid his tiny refrigerator for beer -- blue and silver cans of Foster's for Greg, bottles of San Miguel for Emiliano, and those tiny Michelob half-bottles for me, all of us ignoring that Budweiser was the island's most popular brew.

As second in command at the Embassy, Greg had a large office with a comfy sofa and chairs. We would sit back, brews in hand, and dissect the events of the day as though the day had been a party we hosted. We excelled in turning minor events into scenes we believed worthy of a

TV sitcom. But, of course, we invented new and better dialog for ourselves. Mary Tyler Moore in the tropics.

Today, though, we discuss the upcoming inauguration, the formal celebration of the island nation's new status with the U.S. I make it clear, but not angrily, that I would have preferred a different arrangement for my country, more of an independent nation status.

Greg clears his throat, a warning that I need not say more, and then says he has a favor to ask.

"Shoot," I tell him.

"I need a pretend girlfriend for that event." His face colors, as if embarrassed to be begging such a favor.

I pause to let what he said make sense. "Me?" I ask.

"Take the gig, "Emiliano tells me.

Greg explains that everyone else will have a real spouse or partner and Mrs. Ambassador will have a fit if she has to deal with seating an uneven number at the table.

Emiliano steps in: "I'm sure your mom will give you the day off. It's for a late luncheon at the Ambassador's residence after the Spanish Wall ceremonies."

"Okay," I say, to Greg, "I'd be pleased to."

He sits back, relieved his problem is solved. Emiliano asks if I've applied for a position with the local government's foreign service or if I have any interest in coming back to work with them.

I shake my head. "I have spoken to them informally," I say, "and they told me they'd like to hire me but are waiting for budget approval to add more staff. Anyway, I'm not sure that's what I want. Plus, I think I should have a graduate degree first."

"Back to Hawaii?" Greg asks.

"Humm," I shrug. "Maybe. Or maybe a Japanese university. My uncle and step-grandmother in Tokyo have offered to pay my tuition. I could live with them, plus my undergraduate grades were good enough to possibly get me a partial scholarship."

"Step-grandmother?" Emiliano gives me a raised eyebrow.

"Yes, my uncle's unofficial step-mother who is a very well-educated woman. She gave me Japanese language instruction when I was there and together, we began a translation project. We are still working on it by mail."

Greg comments that a degree from a prestigious Japanese university could open many doors.

"My other choice," I say, "is to continue working here and eventually take over from my mother. I'm not sure I really want to work in the foreign service." "Greg," I turn to him, "you really have no say in decision making, do you? Even the Ambassador gets his marching orders from higher up."

"Welcome to the real world," he replies and then stands. "I've got to get back," he says. Emiliano looks up and nods says he'll see him back at the office. "Soon," he promises. Greg leaves as he got what he needed: a date for the luncheon.

Emiliano leans forward. "Seriously," he says, "you want to throw your education away?"

I shrug. "I can always change my mind," I tell him. "Besides, I'd like to be more involved with my own community, my own island and its future."

"Wow," he says with a big smile. "Deep thinking going on. And now that Landau is gone, I have to tell you that the man you once asked about will be here for the ceremony."

I catch my breath. "Why?" I ask.

Emiliano explains my father will be a member of the delegation representing the U.S. President. To my puzzled look, he adds, "Yes, he was that important during the late days of the Trust Territories and the status negotiations."

I nod my thanks for the information. "We must talk again," he tells me. "I really want to hear more about your new thinking." Before standing, he gives my arm an affectionate squeeze. "I have to get back," he says.

Not long after I returned home, I found a

spare hour to go to the Land Office where I asked about the particular piece of property below Waterfront Road where I had lived with my grandmother.

It took a while for the man to search through the bowels of the back storeroom. He finally returned with an old ledger and then carefully turned the pages. After finding what he was looking for, he returned to the storeroom and came back with yet another ledger.

Finally, he told me. "The land below that part of the waterfront road was created with fill by the Japanese. Since the property did not exist before that, the fill land was considered Japanese government land, and after the war the U.S. Navy took possession."

The man then retrieved yet another ledger from the back and consulted it. "The ownership of that particular piece of property after the war," he said, "was granted to Armina Uchida." He added he heard there was a small hotel on that property and the building had been one of few that survived the

American bombings.

He closed the ledger, then, looking over the top of his glasses told me that during Japanese times that particular area below waterfront had been the entertainment district, mostly tea houses and brothels.

I nodded, and then asked, "who is the current owner of the property?" He consulted his ledger, then retreated again to the back room, and returned with yet another ledger. Slowly he turned the pages.

"As I told you, in 1947, a woman named Armina Uchida laid claim to the property, and she was assigned it by the U.S. Navy who was supervising all the former Japanese state property."

"And then?" I asked.

He looked back at the ledger. "In 1973," he said, "the property was conveyed to Valerio Johnson."

He closed the ledger. I thanked him and left. That was the year my mother married Valerio and the year Armina and I moved to their house on the estuary.

My mother closes her place on the day of the inaugural celebration. All government offices are closed, schools and college have cancelled classes. The three of us: me, my mother, and Loha, have come to watch the ceremonies and listen to the speeches, along with a large number of the town's population. In the Spanish Wall park, stadium seating has been set up for the dignitaries, along with a stage and podium.

The printed program gives the names of those who will be speaking, and the districts of the traditional dance performers, but it does not give the names of the foreign dignitaries attending. I wonder if my mother will recognize the man after all these years. Time takes a toll on the faces and shapes of humans, and I expect he is no longer the handsome man my mother once knew.

A wide area has been cleared in front as

space for the dancers, so most of those sitting behind the podium are a blur. I look around but I am not surprised when I do not see Claire, as hospital workers can't up and leave their jobs. Exceptions are made for heads of departments, as I see Salvador sitting with the dignitaries behind the podium. Valerio must be around somewhere, though I don't see him. The American dignitaries are way in the back, in the shade and shadow. Evidently none will be speaking.

We in the audience stand in the hot sun. My mother at least thought to wear a hat. We listen to the drone of speeches, interspersed with native dance performers. One routine from a neighboring island brings guffaws and tittering behind hands. For those who understand that dialect, the lyrics must be highly risqué. So many islands, so many dialects, some easy, some difficult.

When the official ceremony is over my mother and sister depart for home. I've driven my own car and Emiliano has promised to drop me back here after the luncheon. I see the small group of Americans, among them a tall man who must be my father. They seem to be waiting for the formal photographs. A small Asian or Eurasian woman is standing next to the man I believe is my father.

Emiliano catches my eye and I wave back timidly. He nods and motions to me to come forward.

When I approach the group, the American Ambassador sees me, pulls me over for a hearty hello, gives me a hug and tells me I am missed. Greg squeezes my shoulders, the closest he can get to a hug. Meanwhile, Emiliano begins to encourage everyone to move to the transportation waiting to take us to the Ambassador's residence, and he sorts us into pairs. Even Emiliano's pretty wife has been drafted for the day and assigned to the President of the American Chamber of Commerce, while Emiliano takes the arm of the small Asian woman who must be the wife of my father. This maneuver opens up a space for me to move forward. I look up as I shake the man's hand and I tell him my name is Helen. Then I put my arm through his and escort him to our assigned official vehicle.

I told neither Emiliano nor Claire the new-found truth about my grandmother. But when Claire asked me over last month for sunset drinks, I did tell her about nagging Valerio for a boat for visiting the reef islands and the nearest atolls. I said I hoped she would join us. Maybe, she said and told me of her plans to visit the southern atolls on the field ship, an excursion to which she, in turn, invited me. I found the idea enticing, especially if the ship stops at the atoll that was the home of my true grandmother's family.

On our second glass of pink gin, she showed me the fancy camera she had recently mail-ordered from the States. She seemed thoroughly engaged with her new hobby and spends her days off walking and photographing.

The film has to be sent to the States for developing and printing, a number of weeks wait for turn around. She showed me the first batch: photos of geckos fucking on the wall of her bathroom, lizards sprinting across her porch railing, failed attempts to capture images of her neighbor's mean dogs, and some excellent portraits of people she has met on her walks.

When I told her about not wanting to work for the government, for neither the U.S. nor my own government, she listened and seemed to understand. About my taking an early morning history class at the community college, she wholeheartedly approved. But she also reminded me that if I become a teacher, I would be working for the government. I wagged my head from side to side as I had not thought of that.

I did not tell her about learning the identity of my father. Nor have I told Salvador about my father or my decision of not joining our government's foreign service. So many secrets. I'll be happy when everything is out in the open.

Keeping it all straight as to who knows what and who doesn't know is making me crazy.

Although Valerio has not yet bought a boat, he rented one for a weekend visit to the nearest atoll. Such a surprise to see how skillfully he swings it through the island's complicated reef channels, then through the pass, and out into deep water where he guns the throttle. I thrill to the bow lifting with the sudden speed. I had hoped we would troll for dinner, but instead, we bought some reef fish at the waterfront market before leaving.

Arriving at the atoll in the early afternoon, Valerio maneuvers us through the narrow passage. Once into the large lagoon, he swings to the right and we pass the first islet with its cluster of small open-sided, palm-roofed structures for visitors. The place is empty. Valerio has gotten permission from the owning family for us to quietly visit. He cruises slowly along the quiet lagoon shore, passing several islets, and finally turns in at a far one with a single structure up on posts. On close inspection, the raised wooden floor is sturdy and the roof's thatching in good enough condition to keep us dry, unless a rainstorm blows in sideways. Loha and I help my mother sluice the platform with buckets of water from the lagoon. It will dry before nightfall. My mother then sits in the sandy shallows to gut and clean the fish we brought. Loha and I splash around, and swim out, but not far. I notice a couple of small hammerheads and call to my mother, advising her to fling the entrails as far out into the water as she can.

Later when Loha and I wade ashore, Valerio sends us into the underbrush in search of kindling. With what we bring him he starts a small fire. We packed a restaurant bucket with charcoal and Valerio adds briquettes to the fire. Charcoal is now on regular order at my mother's restaurant since we acquired a few hibachis for grilling the *teriyaki* on a stick. Here we used some coral knobs to form a small fire circle. They appeared to have been used before by other campers.

Valerio himself cooks the fish, laying them on the oven shelf we fetched from our own stove, and my mother brings side dishes from the cooler. We eat with our fingers. My family is intact, and I have learned to appreciate them, all of them. I long to encourage my mother and Valerio to take a vacation. Lena and I, along with the rest of the regular staff, will soon be capable of running Maria's Place for the length of their vacation.

For that reason, I'm anxious for Mieko's book to be published. I want my mother learning about Mieko as I did, by reading her own words. I'm hoping my parents will choose to visit Japan, staying with Uncle Shige and Rose. I've told my mother how important Rose is to me, and how much her house reminded me of the *ryokan* where she and I grew up, the house which I now know was once a brothel. I pass by it when I go to a certain store that carries inexpensive Japanese cookware and such. Grandmother's *ryokan* has become a low-down, by the hour, hotel. And

Valerio the landlord. Oh, well.

As the four of us sit around the dying embers, my mother reminisces. She tells us about her mother going out to the reef flats with Gustof when he went fishing. She reminds us that fishing with men was not something women did, not in those days, and adds that Gustof's death ended her mother's ocean excursions. Me, I'm paying special attention. Mieko wrote about two visits to the ocean with Gustof, but my mother is saying he continued to take her after they moved into town.

"Did you ever go with them?" I ask.

"Once or twice," she says, "but usually I stayed home with Santa."

Before sunset, the sky becomes grey. The normally brilliant exit of the sun is dull, and the light goes in a wink. We douse the fire, pull the boat across the beach and up into the underbrush, turn it over onto its side, and stow the cooler and charcoal bucket under the wooden platform. Valerio and my mother curl up together, as do Loha and I. Our bedding is nothing more than some roughly woven sheets and beach towels. In the wee hours of the morning, rain wets the thatched roof and I suspect we are all having a rather sleepless night on that hard platform.

Still, for me, it was a good sleepless night of thinking. I had not told my father I was his daughter. I tried to keep my conversation during the luncheon at the Ambassador's residence to the usual fluff and chit-chat, a skill I had learned from being a necessary extra at other official Embassy events. Perhaps I allowed myself some freedoms, but Greg was safely at the other end of the table and if he sent me an evil eye, I could easily ignore it. Later in the afternoon, out on the residence *lanai*, my father handed his camera to someone and had him take our picture: his wife, himself and me. Behind us the sky was just beginning to be painted by the setting sun.

He then reached into his jacket pocket for pen and paper, asked for and wrote down my full name and PO address, telling me he would send me a copy of the photo. He also suggested we could write to each other. Does he suspect? Maybe, maybe not.

Now, at the first hint of dawn, I am out on the sand, my feet in the warm water at the lagoon's edge where I'm greeted by a rainbow arching from horizon to horizon. I call to the others to hurry out, although here in the islands such rainbows are not that rare, nor do I read this rainbow as a particular portent of anything. Yet, I'm convinced it was Gustof taking Mieko on those visits to the ocean that impelled her to stay on here and not return to her Japanese homeland.

We did not arrive home until late Sunday, and Monday morning, as usual, I march off to my world history class. After, on the way from the school to my mother's place, I stop at the Post Office. Opening my box, I find a letter from Rose and an envelope stamped "Do Not Bend." The enclosed note says, "Enjoyed meeting you and our conversation during the luncheon. Please, write to me," and signed with just his given name.

I study the photo of my father sandwiched between me and his wife. I'm guessing she is American Chinese, and so tiny. I towered over her. She and I spoke briefly, me crouching with bent knees and leaning down. In the photo the late afternoon is only beginning to bloom a sunset. The three of us look sleepy-eyed after the long lunch and a couple of drinks. Do he and I look alike? Not really, although perhaps there is something similar in shape of our chins and our posture? No, we do not look alike. But neither do I look much like my mother. I have a sudden unwanted thought: what if he sees me as just another dreamy *Bali Ha'i* girl? I shrug. Of course, I will write to him.

CHARACTERS

Armina, native wife of the engineer and mother of Maria, from *Miss Gone-overseas*

Claire, American ex-pat who works in administration at the hospital

Emiliano Welter, administrative local hire at US embassy

Geneva, US Dept of Interior employee on short-time assignment to island

Greg Landau, American diplomat at the US embassy

Hayden, local child adopted by Howard and Sylvia

Helen, born 1963, daughter of Maria and Valerio's stepdaughter

Howard Olson, American doctor assigned to local hospital

Jason Tovar, American tourist who commits suicide

Leialoha, or **Loha**, born 1973, daughter of Maria and Valerio

Maria, born **Mariko** in 1944, daughter of Armina and the engineer, from *Miss Gone-overseas*

Mercedes, wife of Salvador

Mieko, from *Miss Gone-overseas*, the ghost who hovers over the whole book

Rose, German/Japanese housekeeper of Helen's Uncle Shige

Salvador, local director of hospital and uncle of Helen

Serlina, wife of Simon and childhood friend of Helen

Shige, born 1936, son of the engineer from *Miss Gone-overseas*

Simon Luke, local Director of State Finance

Sylvia, American wife of Howard Olson

Valerio, local Director of State Tourism and husband of Maria

TERMS

Banh mi, Vietnamese sandwich

Dashi, Japanese cooking stock

Fusuma, sliding door panels

Futon, Japanese roll up mattress bed

Hai-Hai, Japanese for yes

Hapa Haole, Islander of mixed ancestry

Hibachis, Japanese small cast iron grill

Kapok, natural fibers pillow stuffing

Lanai, porch

Lava-lava, sarong, wrap around skirt

Lavash, unleavened bread
Lei, Hawaiian flower neck garland
Liana, woody vine
Mokilese, Micronesian language
Mwarmwar, flower head garland
Netsuke, Japanese miniature sculptures
Pachinko, mechanical games arcade
Ramen, Japanese noodle soup
Ryokan, Traditional Japanese inn
Saimin, Hawaiian noodle soup
Shoji, Japanese rice paper covered sliding doors
Soba, Japanese buckwheat noodles
Tatami, Japanese rush grass mats
Teriyaki, Japanese cooking technique
Ylang-Ylang, fragrant tropical tree
Zori, Japanese sandal

ABOUT THE AUTHOR

For a number of years in the early 1980s, Mitchell Hagerstrom lived and worked on the island of Pohnpei in Micronesia where these stories take place. As a child, Mitchell lived for a time in Japan and Hawaii. She has lived and worked in Southern California, San Francisco, Missouri, Washington, D.C., and Louisiana. Mitchell now lives in Austin, Texas.

In the past, Mitchell's works have been published in *The Pacific Review,* Spring 1983, *Latte, The Essence of Guam* magazine, February and March 1996.

For more information visit her at the *Miss Gone-overseas* pages on Facebook, Goodreads, and Amazon.